Additional Praise for
THE **Tarantula** WhiSPERER

"With humor and insight, Dr. Pasten wonderfully weaves common sense, understanding and compassion into responsible animal care. This book is invaluable both to people and to the animals in their lives."

> —**Dr. Elliot Katz, D.V.M.**, president, In Defense of Animals

"A terrific, fun, and honest look at the world's best profession. If you love animals as Dr. Pasten and I do, you won't be able to put this book down."

> —**Jeff Werber, D.V.M.**, small animal practitioner, host, Animal Planet's *Petcetera,* veterinary medical correspondent, *CBS News*

"Through the author's caring heart and skill as a veterinarian, readers of this informative and entertaining book will be able to enter the deeper realms of animal understanding and appreciation."

> —**Dr. Michael W. Fox**, author, veterinarian, senior bioethics scholar, The Humane Society of the United States

# THE Tarantula WhiSPERER

## A Celebrity Vet Shares Her Secrets to Communicating with Animals

### DR. LAURA PASTEN

*Foreword by Stephanie Laland*

CONARI PRESS
Berkeley, California

Conari Press books are distributed by Publishers Group West.

From *The Tellington T-Touch* by Linda Tellington. Copyright © 1992 by Linda Tellington-Jones and Sybil Taylor. Illustrations copyright © 1992 by Viking Penguin, a division of Penguin Books USA Inc. Used by permission of Viking Penguin, a division of Penguin Putnam Inc.

Cover illustraton and book design: Suzanne Albertson
Cover art directon: Ame Beanland

ISBN: 1-57324-159-8

*Library of Congress Cataloging-in-Publication Data*
Pasten, Laura.
The tarantula whisperer : a celebrity vet shares her secrets to communicating with animals / Laura Pasten : foreword by Stephanie Laland.
p.     cm.
Includes bibliographical references. (191).
ISBN 1-57324-159-8
1. Pasten, Laura.   2. Pets Anecdotes.   3. Human-animal communication Anecdotes.   4. Veterinarians—United States Biography.   I. Title.

| | |
|---|---|
| SF613.P35A3    1999 | 99–24541 |
| 636.088'7—dc21 | CIP |

Printed in the United States of America on recycled paper
99  00  01  02  03    Data Repro    10  9  8  7  6  5  4  3  2  1

THIS BOOK IS DEDICATED TO TYBO, my Standard Schnauzer, who whispers wisdom through heavenly whiskers. May he enjoy this book while he is waiting for me to cross the Rainbow Bridge with him—we will then be together, never to be separated again.

# THE Tarantula WhiSPERER

# Foreword

The thought of whispering sweet nothings in a tarantula's ear was not immediately appealing to me when I first received a copy of this book. And I was doubtful that a spider might have anything but "You murderer!" to hiss back at me. However, I began to consider whether the day might ever arrive when I would want to commune with an arachnid. Perhaps the thought form "Go away" could be useful. To illustrate the extent of my feelings, a few years ago my husband watched the movie *Arachnophobia* on video, and I managed to sit on the couch next to him through the entire movie, sorting bills, without ever once looking at the screen.

Still, it was an intriguing thought. I had heard that certain yogis can keep mosquitoes from biting them simply by surrounding themselves with thought forms that make the air around them impervious to insects. And so, I gamely decided to give the book a try.

And what a delightful and informative book it turned out to be. Full of humor and sound advice on how to communicate with any animal (not just spiders) by using a healthy combination of intuition and common sense, *The Tarantula Whisperer* delighted me with the true exploits of an animal-loving and practical joke-playing veterinarian whose knack for reading not only the animals in her care but their guardians as well often kept both from harm.

In a breezy and entertaining manner, Dr. Laura Pasten provides tips on subjects as varied as what to do if your companion animal gets a bee sting and how to test if a puppy's personality makes him the right dog for you. And what a relief to hear the good news that common sense can be your greatest ally in figuring out how to care for your animal. Like the dyslexic insomniac who stayed up all night worrying if there is a Dog, we sometimes make things more complicated than they need be.

Animal communication can be fun, intriguing, and eminently practical. Both you and your animals, be they feathered, finned, or furry, will be glad you found this book.

—Stephanie Laland, author of *Animal Angels* and
*Peaceful Kingdom: Random Acts of Kindness by Animals*

# Talk and They
# Will Listen

But now ask the beasts and let them teach you,
And the birds of the air and let them tell you,
Or speak to the earth and let it teach you,
And let the fish of the sea recount to you,
Which among these does not know that the hand
    of the Lord has done this,
And whose hand is the life of every living thing,
    and the breath of all human beings.

*—Job 12:7–10*

I was reading *The Horse Whisperer* by Nicholas Evans recently, and this passage jumped out at me: "For secrets uttered softly into pricked and troubled ears, these men were known as Whisperers. Horse whisperers could see into the creature's soul and soothe the wounds they found there. . . ."

It was then I realized that I'm a Whisperer, too. As a veterinarian, I have received a great deal of medical training and know how to treat all kinds of esoteric diseases. But when it comes right down to it, most of the time I just listen to an animal and somehow know what to do. That's why, in much of my veterinary practice, I really just use common sense. And much of what I teach human guardians about interacting with their companion animals and keeping them healthy is pure common sense too.

Now I realize that common sense isn't as "common" as it use to be, and that to be a Whisperer you must combine common sense with understanding, appreciation, and knowledge of the animal you're dealing with. Most people love and cherish their animals, but haven't learned how to communicate with them. But I've come to believe that we can all learn how to talk to them and have a deeper communion with the animals with whom we share our lives.

Communicating with animals has become a bigger and bigger issue as companion animals have become a vital part of many of our lives. Indeed, many animals have even attained the status of family members. Groucho Marx said, "Outside of a dog, a book is man's best friend. Inside of a dog, it's too dark to read." Seriously, though, companion animals are becoming more and more important to our mental and emotional health. Americans own more than 50 million dogs and over 60 million cats. We now spend more than twice as much each year on animal food as on baby food. (A sickening testimony to the close identity we have with our companion animals can be found in history. When the Nazis marched into Austria, they killed all the dogs they found in the homes of Jews, on the grounds that they were "Jewish" dogs. Let's pray humanity never cannibalizes its children, two-legged or four-, in such an evil and senseless manner again.)

Animals have a great deal to teach us, and in these pages I share some of the wisdom and humor that my patients—some feathered, some furred, and some scaled—have taught me. (I hope some congressmen and congresswomen are reading this book; if more of them had horse sense, we'd have a more "stable" government.) I also want to offer some animal lore not widely known, as well as practical advice for common problems that can plague companion animals and their guardians but can be dealt with at home simply if you just know how. All the stories recounted here actually occurred in my practice.

**3**

You will notice that just as with humans, some animals are wise, and some "other" wise. Some of the communication techniques might seem foreign to you, but remember what the caterpillar said to the butterfly: "You'll never get me up in one of those things."

Before we get started, keep in mind that some of the most important forms of communication are not verbal, and that using common sense and intuition can also be effective in communicating with people. An incident from my junior year of veterinary school illustrates this point.

When I was in veterinary school, there were eight women in my class—the most women, by far, in the history of veterinary medicine to that point. (Now, incoming classes are over half women.) Professors were still getting use to the idea that women could be just as good (or better) veterinarians as men. Some large animal medicine professors in particular didn't believe women could handle horses and livestock (forgetting that the difference in strength between a 160-pound man and a 125-pound woman really wasn't significant with a 1,000-pound horse—in both cases dealing successfully with the horse required animal tranquilizers and human skill rather than brute strength). These "old school" professors often created obstacles or hardships for women—sort of a "rights of passage." I had one of these men for Large Animal Ambulatory Medicine, which is a class where a professor and four students drive out to ranches for veterinary calls on large animals.

An important part of livestock medicine is performing necropsies (the equivalent of autopsies in humans) to determine why the animals died. It is not uncommon for a rancher to come across a cow that had died days earlier. (This isn't a pretty sight, so if you have a queasy stomach, skip ahead a page.) In the 100-degree weather of Davis, California, these cows (being ruminants) would bloat up like macabre balloons, and the stench and flies around the corpse would turn the stomachs of even the most seasoned veterinarians. It soon became obvious that I was being singled out to do the necropsies on all the maggoty, putrid cases. So that you can empathize, let me describe how one does a necropsy on such a huge animal.

You put on coveralls, boots, mask (which still allows you to smell all too keenly), and gloves. You roll the animal on its back and make an incision from its neck to its abdomen. Due to the size of a cow, you can't see all of the organs clearly by merely peering in—you have to step *into* the abdominal cavity and carefully examine all of the organs for clues as to why the animal died.

So, back to our dead cow that has been simmering in the hot sun for several days. The carcass has been covered with swarms of flies for days—enough time for their larva to hatch; there are now waves of wiggling maggots. It is almost impossible not to vomit from the potent smells of spoiled meat. Climbing into the carcass saturates your coveralls with blood. As you inspect the organs, you have to constantly flick flies off your face. Get the picture?

When three times in a row I was singled out to do the procedure (while the three male students were off vaccinating sheep or worming horses), I said that I thought it was someone else's turn. Met with stony silence, I meekly proceeded with my hellish chore.

The fourth time, I proclaimed confidently, "I've already done several; I wouldn't want to deprive another student from learning how to do these." My thinly disguised whine fell on deaf ears, so I again was forced to perform this nauseating chore. Clearly I wasn't communicating with my professor.

The next day—you guessed it—another bloated cow for me. But *this* time I was prepared. This time, I beamed with enthusiasm, and thanked him for the opportunity, because I had learned so much from the previous four necropsies. I promptly donned a rubber scuba diving outfit (impermeable to body fluids) and scuba mask (which allowed me to breathe through my mouth, but which was airtight to smell). Making my incision, I climbed into the foul body cavity.

"Sir," I said peering intently at a semiliquid liver. "What does this blemish on the liver represent?"

The professor had to hold his breath and lean into the fly-ridden cavity to respond.

The moment he finished answering, I drew his attention to the intestinal contents. "Sir, does the consistency of this feces suggest parasites?" Again, he had to stick his head into the fetid remains.

I continued asking questions requiring his close inspection. Suddenly a look of realization crossed his face. It was at that moment that we finally communicated. Without the exchange of a sound or gesture between us, each had perfectly understood the other—our minds and hearts were properly attuned. I was never asked to do another necropsy on a dead cow.

There wasn't anything "bookish" or scientific about this communication; it was merely common sense. And once you understand what motivates animals and how they think, you can apply common sense in interacting with them, too.

First, let's talk about common sense (as opposed to horse sense, which is what keeps horses from betting on what people will do). I guess it's fairly obvious that to make sense out of anything, we must put some sense into it. To listen to animals, we need to use *all* of our senses in novel ways. If you want to be a Whisperer, you have to learn to:

Listen with your fingers.

See with your gut.

Think with your heart.

I remember watching an old TV show where Archie Bunker said to his wife, Edith: "The reason you don't understand me is because I'm talkin' to you in English and you're listenin' in Dingbat." Fortunately, we don't need a Berlitz language course for animals, we merely need to understand or realize what they understand, feel what they feel, and see what they see. One big obstacle to understanding, feeling, and seeing as animals do is our concept of animals as "lesser beings." Because we believe them to be inferior to us, while we love them, we generally feel we must dominate them. But we need to *understand,* not dominate (and *understanding* does not mean both of you understanding that you are the boss—although having others eat out of your hand does save a lot of dish washing).

*Understanding* is the key word here. Many times, we think we are communicating, but we aren't, because we didn't see the situation from the other person's or animal's viewpoint. One such misunderstanding happened to one of my clients.

Mrs. Mazur had a Miniature Schnauzer; hair from his eyebrows kept growing into his eyes and causing inflammation. Her dog was too lively for her to cut his hair herself, so she came to my office every two weeks for a trim. After several months, she asked in desperation, "Isn't there anything I can do to stop the hair from growing back so quickly?"

I said, "Yes, you can go to the pharmacy and get some Nair for hair removal. Bring it with you on your next visit, and we'll apply it to the area for you."

Mrs. Mazur was pleased with the suggestion, and immediately drove to a pharmacy. She asked the druggist for some Nair. The pharmacist got a bottle, and as he handed it to her, he said, "If you apply it to your underarms, don't apply deodorant for several hours."

Mrs. Mazur said, "It isn't for my underarms."

The pharmacist then said, "Well, if you apply it to your legs, don't wear panty hose for two days."

"It isn't for my legs; it's for my Schnauzer."

"Oh, well in that case, don't ride a bicycle for two weeks," the pharmacist replied helpfully.

Yes, with animals, just as with people, we must try to avoid misunderstandings. And sometimes it's very difficult to tell what's wrong; we just know that something isn't right (like a hearse with white sidewalls). We must try to see things from the animal's point of view. And we must not assume a superior attitude to *any* member of the animal kingdom.

Often we are arrogant concerning our special powers and place in evolution. But we did not evolve to be any more special than our fellow animals. We can't jump 130 times our height like a flea; run as fast as a cheetah; smell as well as a dog; hear with radar like a bat; live as long as a tortoise (200 years); we can't even walk upside down on the ceiling like a spider or fly.

When thinking about other creatures—whether they are dogs and horses, or rattlesnakes, spiders, and roaches—we should remember what naturalist Henry Beston said: "The animal shall not be measured by man. In a world older and more complete than ours, they move finished and complete, gifted with extensions of the senses we have lost or never attained. . . . They are not underlings: they are other nations, caught with ourselves in the net of life and time, the splendor and travail of the earth." My philosophy is not to think that creatures are inferior to humans, but that they are unique *from* us—and to enjoy that uniqueness.

J. Allen Boone, who made human-animal communication his life work, concluded that animals often behave the way people expect them to behave. He believed that if you think a certain animal—like a house-fly, for example—is a pest, then it will act like a pest. But if you accept and respect the housefly (because it comes from the same universal source as people), and you can admire it, say, for its ability to fly or for the delicacy of its body, it will stop being a pest. Boone proved to researchers that he could communicate with a fly, whom he named Freddie. Freddie actually came when silently called, and, when requested, refrained from walking on Boone's bare skin. (No, he didn't shoo him; he let him go barefooted.)

Mark Twain says that for a doctrine to last forever, it must be humorous as well as teach and preach. So this book will attempt to do just that—teach and preach using humor.

Remember that the only medicine that needs no prescription, has no unpleasant taste, and costs no money is laughter. Doctors now say that cheerful people resist disease better than grumpy ones—sort of the surly bird catches the germ theory.

Ready? Let's all become Whisperers! ☀

# Lend Me Your Ear

**M**y receptionist said there was a phone call I definitely should take. I grimaced—I was already way behind—but I went to the phone. "Hello, this is Dr. Pasten. How can I help you?"

"This is Mr. Stevenson," said the caller. His voice sounded on edge. "My pet tarantula, Harry, was walking around on my shirt, like he usually does. But he got to my ear he hunched down like they do when they're mad, and I can't get him off. What do I do?" You could hear his panic.

Now, there is nothing I detest more than spiders—I can't squash them fast enough. I believe spiders are the type of creatures you kill the instant you see them, not only for your own good, but for the protection of your fellow man. Just thinking of Harry attached to the guy's ear was giving me goose bumps.

I reviewed what I knew about tarantulas. Tarantulas are like little ballerinas, walking around on the tips of their toes. When they get upset—scared or mad—they crouch down and dig in with their little barbed feet. If you further provoke them, they'll give a vicious bite—not a good thing on a person's ear or head. If Mr. Stevenson tried to pry him off, he most certainly would get bitten. But he had already waited a long time, and the tarantula hadn't budged. What could I suggest—, besides referring him to someone—anyone—else?

"I'm really not certain, to tell the truth," I said. "But if it were me, I'd stick my head in the refrigerator. Either the cold temperature will encourage him to get up and walk away, or the hypothermia will slow him down enough so you might be able to pry him off your ear without getting bitten. But there's no way I can go back to work without knowing what happens to you. Please, let me hold. Come back and tell me what happened."

"Okay," he said with hesitation.

Long moments passed. Clients waiting in rooms kept stepping out and gesturing angrily at their watches. I smiled apologetically and prayed that Mr. Stevenson would be both lucky and speedy. It seemed like he was gone for ages.

When he came back on the phone, I immediately heard the relief in his voice. "It worked! I stuck my head in the refrigerator, and he uncurled from my ear and started walking down my shirt where I could grab him!"

So, now you, too know how to get a tarantula off your ear. . . .

の 9の 9の 9の

How did I know the tarantula would let go when cold? I'm not sure—I guess, because I'm a *Tarantula Whisperer*. Dave Barry talks about the existence of a Betty Crocker gland somewhere in people that secretes a hormone that enables you to sew curtains or decorate. He says there must also be a Mr. Goodwrench gland to allow you to fix things, and that our inabilities in any of these areas must be due to a deficiency in a gland's secretions. It would be helpful if there were a Saint Francis gland to help us communicate with the animals, but it really isn't necessary.

As children, we start out with minds that are open and flexible, but as we grow older it becomes more and more difficult to have beliefs that are beyond our cultural definitions of reality. In our "prove-it-to-me" scientific society we say we don't believe in "the supernatural," preferring to acknowledge as "natural" only that which can be explained logically.

Native people around the world have always understood that all of life is interconnected in a vast network and have known to tap into it for communication. To Native Americans, nothing is "supernatural" or beyond Nature, because nothing, including themselves, is apart from it. They think it perfectly "natural" to be able to hear in their own minds the thoughts of plants and animals. And don't forget—being natural isn't dominating. (It's not Adam saying to Eve, "Hey! I wear the plants in this family!")

    ◈ ◈ ◈ ◈ ◈

Human beings are like tacks; they can go only as far as their heads will let them. So, use your "image-ination." Imagine thinking of the animals as equal beings that you admire for their positive traits (their cleverness, their pretty colors, their ability to adapt) and ask them to be partners with you. Be sure and communicate with a specific animal. A communication addressed "To whom it may concern" usually gets to someone whom it doesn't concern.

Thoughts are things. The brain emits electrical energy—that's what an EEG records. Projected thought-things are forces. Imagine telling the raccoon that you think he is very clever and resourceful, but would he please leave your garbage can alone. "Image-in" him walking past your garbage can without disturbing it. Be prepared though—your neighbors might hate you when the raccoon ambles next door. See the world through a "beginner's mind." Try to imagine new ways of communicating and viewing things. Try to be like the baby mouse walking through a cave who said to his mother when a bat flew by, "Look Mama, an angel!"

Barbara Woodhouse was a brilliant dog trainer. She could take any dog and have it focused on her every word. She subscribed to the four "Fs" in dog training: fun, fair, firm, and focus. By focusing or picturing in her mind's eye a dog happily doing exactly what she wanted, she believed she was showing the dog what she literally "had in mind."

We have to develop a mental bridge with animals, not as an intelligent person to a dumb creature but as equal to equal, a bridge for two-way, not one-directional, thought traffic. (Remember the old adage: Marriage is a dialogue; divorce is two monologues. We need a dialogue here.)

As Whisperers, when we communicate with the animals, we need to "listen" to our insights. God gave us two ears and only one mouth—to remind us to listen more than talk. (It's been said that if we did a better job of listening, history wouldn't have to repeat itself.)

Francis of Assisi has been an inspiration for many people, especially those who are interested in Nature. He saw all creatures as his brothers and sisters. He had the knack of communicating friendliness and confidence to animals through his body language. (Remember, Francis tamed the wild wolf of Gubbio in much the same way that Daniel communicated with the lions in the den—by sensitive body language.) He knew the way to approach an animal so that it would perceive the intruder as a friend, not a threat. By his inner attitude, he unified the world of animals and man.

"Listen" to Mother Nature. Why do you think they refer to Nature as a woman? No, it's not because they can't find out how old it is. At the dawn of man's existence on Earth, woman healers learned to harmonize with the laws of Nature.

They obtained much of their information from the careful observance of Nature itself. Diane Stein in *Natural Healing for Dogs and Cats* describes this observance of Nature well. She points out that healers noticed that a wounded deer would lie quietly in a bed of special ferns until the bleeding ceased; hence, they learned of the plant's special anti-coagulant properties. They watched as a mongoose bitten by a venomous snake ran to some plantain and rubbed it on the poisoned site, thereby living to fight yet another battle. They recognized the healing touch of a mother's tongue on a newborn. They learned that everything connects to everything else, and holistic medicine was born.

We have become removed from this closeness with the Earth. Few have helped a ewe to lamb or a mare to birth her foal (or even seen a human birth). Few have spent the night in a barn watching over an animal in a healing crisis. Our lives are far less intertwined with Nature, animals, and the smaller lives around them.

In Western medicine, we view both our bodies and our companion animals' bodies as being primarily physical, material objects—almost machines. Accordingly, when we consider causes of disease we look almost exclusively to physical ones, like germs or parasites "invading" from outside. It is therefore not surprising that orthodox medicine generally treats symptoms like an enemy, which must be controlled and suppressed. Yet in most cases symptoms represent the action of the individual's vital force, which attempts to throw off the disturbance through diarrhea, vomiting, coughing, sneezing, or pus and scab formation. Nature gives us a biological clock; Western doctors give painkillers or medicine to turn off the alarm. Western doctors love to use "wonder drugs." Every time they "wonder" what's wrong, they give antibiotics or cortisone. Holistic therapies, by contrast, tend to work with the action of the symptoms, gently helping the body in its attempt to restore harmony.

As Michael W. Fox, vice president of the Humane Society of the United States, said, "Holistic medicine respects and is attuned to the 'wisdom of the body.' This body wisdom—the connection between body-sensitivity and mind awareness—has almost been lost to modern civilization, which separates mind from body, man from animal, and humanity from nature. We have to relearn the fact that our bodies are not machines, nor are animals." ❀

# Teri the Terrible

nother one of my clients had a tarantula named Teri (maybe I should move my practice to another neighborhood) who was particularly big and hairy. (Keep in mind that I think tarantulas make lousy companions. Even the best-trained, most intelligent, and most loyal tarantulas tend to look and behave very much like ordinary common-criminal spiders.) The man was certain Teri was lonely, so he asked my advice about getting another tarantula. I called the local pet store and learned that it would be okay if the man got another tarantula of about the same size. He bought another one and the next day he called me, none too pleased. Within five minutes of his introducing the new tarantula, Teri pounced on it, then killed and devoured it, leaving behind only the poison sac.

"Hmmm," I said, "I guess Teri wasn't lonely; he was hungry."

෧෨෧෨෧෨

Thinking of tarantulas, I'm reminded that dogs often get painful and even dangerous insect bites. They result in red, painful swellings, and anaphylactic or allergic reactions can be very serious. A good thing to carry in your animal's travel kit (or your own emergency kit) is meat tenderizer such as Accent. Meat tenderizer works by breaking down protein. When you add a little water to make a paste, you can put it on a painful insect bite; it will break down much of the toxin that is causing the pain. In Hawaii, all emergency personnel carry meat tenderizer. They use it for the toxins on the skin from fire coral, and for centipede and other insect bites. Residents often use ground-up papaya if they are out of meat tenderizer—apparently the enzymes in papaya are similar in their action.

In Hawaii, I learned a helpful hint regarding creatures such as centipedes. It seems that many people get stung or bitten while trying to kill them, and that in hotel rooms centipedes often escape while people are looking for something to kill them with, causing a restless night for the occupants. I've seen people in similar dilemmas—their dog is attacking a centipede and the owner can't restrain the dog plus find something suitable for killing the centipede. What you need to know is that creatures such as centipedes and scorpions are pressure tactile; that is, they move until they feel pressure both on top and bottom, then they feel safe. Therefore, when you see a centipede, throw a shirt or towel on it— it will feel pressure from the cloth plus the ground or floor and remain stationary until you decide what to do with it.

But back to insect bites (bee stings, spider bites, and so on). Besides using meat tenderizer, applying a freshly sliced onion on your dog or cat can help. Or you can rub in a drop of ammonia (used as a cleaning agent for windows or floors). If your dog gets a bee sting, you can scrape with the *dull* or back side of a knife back and forth across the area of the sting a few times. This will grab the stinger and pull it out without pain. Do not try to grab a stinger with your fingers or with tweezers, as this will squeeze more poison into the wound. ☀

**Even a Bird Knows You
Shouldn't Talk Until
a Lawyer Is Present**

**M**rs. Lawson continued to talk to Pierre, her white cockatoo, as the receptionist filled out the paperwork to board Pierre with us for a week.

"Say 'Pretty Boy.' 'Pretty Boy.' Come on, Pierre, talk for Mama. Say 'Pretty Boy . . . Pretty Boy.'" She peered into the cage, her eyebrows knitted together in a frown, "Why do you not talk to me? Why do you not talk to me?" Pierre just sat on his perch—calm and quiet. Mrs. Lawson shook her head and turned to leave, shoulders rounded and head bent, muttering something about Pierre being the only bird she hadn't been able to teach to talk. It reminded me of the adage that for a bird, talk is "Cheep."

Mrs. Lawson had requested that Pierre be on his perch in the waiting room during the day and in his cage at night. Pierre was a star boarder, never causing any problems and barely making a peep, although almost everyone tried to get Pierre to talk to them. They'd twist their head from side to side and in baby voices say things like, "Hello. Can you say, Hello?" "Pretty bird" or "What's your name?" Pierre would always stare back in silence, showing no interest in anyone or anything except his sunflower seeds.

One afternoon I was in the treatment room, when I saw a little Chihuahua run by. (It turned out that the Chihuahua belonged to an attorney who, while he went to the restroom, left his little dog alone in the waiting room.) The dog's little tan body was a blur, but I could see that its tail was tucked between his legs, and he looked scared to death. I heard a sound—kind of a plop, plop, plop sound. What the? . . .

Then I saw the cockatoo on the floor waddling after the dog as quickly as his little feet could go . . . plop, plop, plop. Pierre was running after the dog, flapping his wings in an effort to gain speed, screeching at the top of his lungs, "Why do you not talk to me? Why do you not talk to me?"

Obviously, Pierre's owner had spent a lot of time trying to communicate with Pierre, but had been unsuccessful. Just think how successful Mrs. Lawson would have been, if she could have communicated her desire for Pierre to speak to her, and if Pierre could have communicated his anxiety, distrust, or misunderstanding of what she was doing.

※ ※ ※ ※ ※

As I've been saying, many people, including myself, truly believe that they can "talk to the animals" and that animals can communicate with us. This is not a special gift of the person or animal trying to communicate—all people and all animals can do it. I'm not referring to body language, although animals do a great job of communicating like that. We've all seen and understood how an animal's body, ear, and tail positions show its mood emotion, and intent. A dog with her head lowered to her chest, ears back, and teeth bared, is a dog that will bite. A cat with her back arched and fur standing on end is ready to attack.

Body language is important, but people and animals can communicate much more directly and with more complex thoughts. Diane Stein, in *Natural Healing for Dogs and Cats,* explains the process of teaching people to think images and "send" them to their companion animals, and vice versa. She also explains how to use these communication techniques for healing and relaxing your animals—even how to perform these methods from distances if your companion is at the veterinary hospital or you are on a trip. (By the way, these techniques are described between guardians and their companion animals, but they obviously work well between people and babies also.) I'll share some of the basics here with you.

Webster says the word *communication* means "the exchange of information." Note the word, *exchange.* This exchange or communication is important with your companion animal. When we learn how to communicate with our animals, we form more meaningful relationships as well as gain the ability to help them heal and feel better.

First, we must be respectful of our companion animals. This is sometimes difficult even for animal lovers. We have been indoctrinated into believing that animals are "below" us intellectually. We have to set this prejudice aside; focus on the value of the animal, whether for beauty, love, or for the function that it performs. Out of this genuine value we perceive for the companion animal will come honest feelings of dignity, worth, and esteem for him. Your animal is very sensitive to the presence of these feelings, and true communication cannot occur trans-species without the animal sensing respect.

It is best to put yourself in a meditative state. Turn off the TV and be in the room alone with the animal. Begin by quietly observing the animal, perhaps whispering terms of endearment and reassurances to him. Concentrate on your breathing—deep breaths in and out, in and out. Try to empty your thoughts—just concentrate on your breathing. Look at your companion animal, focus gently upon him, and let other distractions slip away. Softly speak the resting dog or cat's name, or touch, rub, or pat him gently to get his attention. Speak to him aloud or in your mind. Your chance of success is greatly magnified if you think in images or pictures—remember animals have a relatively limited vocabulary in English—so transmit thoughts in a series of still-life pictures. You might transmit a picture of your companion animal sitting, your giving the command, "Stay," and the animal waiting for your return and you praising him. You might picture him starting to chew on a shoe, then changing his mind, and you praising him.

Although most animals respond better to pictures than words, the combination of both makes for clearer communication. Keep it simple, with the words and pictures (visualizations) sending the same message. After sending a message, observe the animal calmly and wait to receive a response. Keep other thoughts and distractions out of your mind, and be open to "hearing" and receiving. The animal's words and pictures will appear in your mind, just as yours were spoken in your mind when you sent them to him. Do not anticipate what your companion animal might say.

Be very careful what you communicate. Depression in human guardians produces depression in companion animals—strong enough to break down their immune systems and cause many pathologies: skin diseases, digestion problems, hypothyroidism, heart, liver, and kidney dysfunctions. As with people, the emotions of anger and resentment are the most destructive. ✳

# Buzzards Circle
# Dead Things—Right?

They brought him wrapped in a towel, like some macabre tortilla. His naked red head and beady eyes glared at me, his huge beak capable of breaking bones larger than mine, ready to strike. It was a buzzard. Apparently, he had the misfortune of landing on some high voltage wires, was electrocuted, and now was paralyzed.

My compassion mounted as I inspected his limp but tightly curled talons. I felt his breast bone; there was hardly any muscle on either side of it—this buzzard was truly emaciated. I had no appropriate food for him, so I offered him canned cat food dipped in a vitamin/mineral powder. He looked at it with utter disdain—obviously it was much too fresh. He needed immediate nutrition, so three of us worked together for half an hour to force feed him and then put him in a cage.

A few minutes later, while passing his cage to retrieve another animal for treatment, we saw him regurgitate all that we had painstakingly fed him. We got him out again and repeated the procedure. Again, after walking by, we saw him again upchuck all our efforts.

Then I remembered something I had read about buzzards. They are heavy, cumbersome birds that gorge themselves on carrion. Their ability to fly after such a heavy meal was seriously compromised, so they evolved a curious habit. When startled by a predator, for example, they involuntarily regurgitate the contents of their stomach, which lightens their weight enough to allow them to fly or flee from danger. Every time we walked by his cage, he was startled, and therefore he regurgitated.

We ended up putting the buzzard in isolation and covering the front of his cage with cardboard so he couldn't see or be seen. This worked well. Our buzzard friend stayed with us two months, gradually reclaiming the use of his limbs. We called him Igor and actually became quite fond of him.

Finally, the day came when he was well enough to be released back into the wild. All of the staff wanted to be present, and his graceful soaring to freedom caused many a misty eye. He circled over the hospital as if to say, "Thank you," and we all congratulated each other on a job well done.

But the next day Igor was still circling over the hospital. He obviously still thought of it as home. The next day there he was again—circling overhead, and the next day as well. I became increasingly agitated—this had to be bad publicity for my animal hospital. After all, buzzards circle dead things—right? To see a buzzard repeatedly circling couldn't exactly elicit trust from my clients.

One of my technicians suggested luring him over to a colleague's hospital by throwing a dead chicken or something into his parking lot. I expressed my indignation, telling her "Only buzzards feed on friends." Fortunately (before I had time to reconsider my assistant's suggestion), in about a week, the buzzard flew off to new hunting grounds.

Everyone would agree that a circling buzzard is bad PR for a veterinary hospital. But what about a black cat? In most of the world, if a black cat crosses your path or enters your house, it is considered unlucky—probably due to its association with medieval occult practices.

Why do most black cats have at least a few white hairs? The reason is a remnant from a disastrous period in the history of European felines. In medieval times, the black cat was associated with black magic and sorcery, and the Christian Church organized annual burning-cats-alive ceremonies on the day of the Feast of Saint John. For these cruel rituals the most wicked and depraved of "Satan's felines" were strongly preferred, and all-black cats were eagerly sought out for the flames. But, in the minds of the pious worshipers, these cats had to be totally black to be really evil. Any touch of white on their black coats was taken as a sign that they did not belong to the Devil. As a result, cats that were totally black became less and less common, while those that were black with a touch of white survived to pass on their genes.

There is an old saying: "Born a black cat, always a black cat." But this isn't true of the Siamese cat. When a Siamese kitten is born, its fur is all white. As it grows, the color begins to change. Dark pigments appear at the tip of its ears and tail and on the pads of its feet. These darkening extremities or "points" slowly spread, and by time the cat is one year old, the adult pattern is seen.

When a Siamese kitten is reared in a very cold environment, it is born all white as usual, but it darkens dramatically as it grows older. Instead of having a pale body with dark points, it becomes dark all over. If raised in an unusually hot environment, the Siamese kitten will develop into an adult that is pale all over, lacking the dark points altogether.

The reason is that, in the Siamese cat, a *lower* skin temperature causes more pigmentation to be laid down in the growing hairs. That is why the newborn kitten, which has a *higher* body temperature, is white all over. Then, as it grows up with a normal, average temperature, the hotter area of its body—its central trunk region—remains pale in color, while its cooler extremities (ear, muzzle, feet, and tip of tail) become gradually darker. Interestingly, if a Siamese cat injures a leg, requiring a bandage, the increased temperature under the wrap can cause all new hairs to be white. A veterinarian has to be very careful about shaving a show Siamese cat—the shaved area, which is cooler due to loss of hair, can turn black.

Even with a healthy Siamese, as the animal grows older, its general body temperature begins to fall slightly, causing its body fur to darken little by little (that's why a Champion Siamese cat's career usually lasts only three or four years). ☀

# The Plainclothes
# Police Dog

A small woman with cherub cheeks proudly set the puppy on the examination table. "I just got him from the animal shelter this morning. Isn't he adorable? What kind of dog do you think he is?"

The little tyke *was* cute. He was black and tan and had perky erect ears. He was growling and playing tug-o-war with the woman's purse. "A German Shepherd . . . a police dog," I said.

"Police dog? He doesn't look like one to me," she said twisting her head from side to side to see him better.

"That's because he's in plain clothes," I said, pausing for raucous laughter. Hearing none, I proceeded. "He *is* special. I can understand why you fell in love with him. Have you named him already?"

"Yeah. . . . Gus. I've always wanted a Gus." She leaned over to kiss Gus, who lunged to bite her nose.

Mrs. Sanders jerked back, but too late. I had to pry Gus' mouth open to rescue her. Mrs. Sanders clutched her nose in agony, tears flowing down her cheeks.

I thumped Gus on the nose. "No! Bad dog!"

"Oh, don't hit him, Doc. He's just a baby. He didn't mean anything," she said lovingly as she scooped him up and cradled him in her arms.

"Sorry, I should have let you discipline him. A German Shepherd is a wonderful breed—very intelligent and loyal, but they do need a master they can respect—an alpha dog, so to speak. As long as you give them plenty of love, they seem to appreciate firm discipline—it almost helps them bond with . . ." I stopped to grab a Kleenex to wipe Mrs. Sanders' hand—trickles of blood from Gus' needle-like baby teeth. "Before you get too attached to this little stinker, why don't we do some tests on him to see what his personality traits are. Let's make sure he's the right dog for you."

The puppy was now struggling and pawing violently in an attempt to get out of her hands. She immediately set Gus down on the floor. I could already tell that Gus was much too dominant a dog for Mrs. Sanders.

"Oh, that won't be necessary. I *know* Gus is right for me!" She leaned down and held out her hands. "Come to Mamma, Gus. Come to Mamma." Gus had found a plastic cap and was busy pouncing on it, totally ignoring her.

"I've developed some quick and easy tests to tell the personality IQ of a dog." Gus was now attacking Mrs. Sanders' shoes. I continued. "Even if you have definitely decided to keep Gus, it would help you know how much obedience training he will need. Want to try it? Wouldn't you like to at least find out how smart Gus is?" I asked.

"Thanks, Doc, but I can tell he's a smart one. Why don't you just check him out and give him his shots."

After the exam and vaccines, I handed her a flyer on a beginning obedience class just starting up. "Be sure and enroll Gus in a puppy class. It'll be fun for both of you."

"That would be fun," she said. As she left the room, I noticed that the flyer was still lying on the table. Oh, well, you can lead a horse to water, but you can't make him drink.

❧ ❧ ❧

I didn't see Gus or Mrs. Sanders for over a year—she hadn't responded to any of my vaccination reminder notices. I assumed she was taking Gus to another veterinarian (maybe one who didn't "bug" her about testing her dog). So, I was surprised when Mrs. Sanders walked into the waiting room.

"Can you come out to the car and get Gus, Doc? He gets nervous coming into veterinary hospitals," she said.

"I think it would be better if we trained Gus not to fear coming in. There will be many procedures we can't do out in the car, so why don't we get him used to coming in? What is he here for?"

"Neutering. My friends have told me that he needs to be neutered. I love him so much, but he's a handful—headstrong, you know. Can someone come out to the car and get him?" she asked timidly.

We were very busy and behind schedule, so I handed her a leash and suggested she bring him in, then I'd have an assistant take him from her. She gave me an odd look, but finally, with slumped shoulders, she proceeded toward the car.

Moments later she rushed into the hospital (without Gus), blood streaming down her hand. It seems Gus had bitten her when she tried to put the leash around his head. "He's very protective of the car," she said apologetically as we bandaged her up.

I went out to the car (none of my assistants would) to get Gus. I opened the door and was greeted with a deep growl—a full-grown German Shepherd with his hackles up. I made a lasso out of the leash and flicked it over his head, tightened it, and pulled him out of the car with a firm, "Come!" I quickly walked toward the hospital, giving a yank on the lead and commanding, "Heel." Gus promptly trotted by my side, giving me no trouble.

Mrs. Sanders was amazed. "How did you do that? He never minds me. Why is he being so good with you?"

"Gus is the type of dog that is both intelligent and dominant. He will only obey someone he feels is more dominant than he is. We'll definitely have to get the two of you enrolled in an obedience class."

I neutered Gus, and called Mrs. Sanders to tell her the surgery was completed, and that Gus did just fine. She asked if she could come right down and pick up Gus while he was still sleepy. I normally keep anesthetized animals over night, but she was insistent, so I relented. She arrived at the hospital; I put Gus in the back seat, and off she drove.

The next day I called Mrs. Sanders to see how Gus was doing.

"Fine, I think," she said.

"Is he eating well and feeling good?"

"Aah . . . aah, well I really don't know," she said.

"What do you mean?"

"Well, you see he growled at me when I tried to get him out. I left the car door open so he could jump out when he was ready. He's still in the car."

This true story indicates how important puppy testing is. I recently produced a video entitled *How Smart Is Your Puppy?* It demonstrates how to give fifteen easy tests to a puppy to determine its intelligence and personality.

One of the tests is called the "short-term memory" test. You let the puppy smell and see a piece of meat, then let him watch you put it behind a box or chair. Distract or play with the puppy for thirty seconds, then see what he does. If he remembers the hidden treat and runs immediately to it, he is very smart; if he sniffs around and takes up to twenty seconds to find it, he's average; if he never looks for it, he's dull (or not food-motivated).

A test I wish I could have convinced Mrs. Sanders to do on Gus when he was a puppy was the "restraint" test. You crouch down and gently roll the puppy on his back and hold him with your hand for thirty seconds. If he struggles fiercely and tries to nip, he is scored 1; if he struggles, then settles down, then struggles again, he is scored 3; if he doesn't struggle and tries to avoid eye contact, he is scored 6.

There are thirteen more tests described in the video. If a puppy scores mostly 1s, the dog is extremely dominant and has aggressive tendencies. He is quick to bite and is generally considered not good with children and elderly people. This is not a dog for the inexperienced handler; it takes a competent trainer to establish leadership.

A dog or puppy scoring mostly 2s is dominant and can be provoked to bite. He will respond well to firm, consistent obedience in an adult household, and is likely to be a loyal companion once he respects his human leader. He often has a bouncy outgoing temperament, but he may be too active for the elderly and too dominant for small children.

If a puppy scores mostly 3s, he accepts humans as leaders easily. He is the best prospect for the average person, adapts well to new situations, and is generally good with children and the elderly, although he may be inclined to be active. He makes a good obedience prospect and usually has a commonsense approach to life.

If a dog or puppy scores mostly 4s, he is submissive and will adapt to most households. He may be slightly less outgoing and active than a dog scoring mostly 3s. He gets along well with children generally and trains easily.

If the dog scores mostly 5s, he is extremely submissive and needs special handling to build confidence and bring him out of his shell. He does not adapt well to change and confusion and needs a very regular, structured environment. He is usually safe around children and bites only when severely stressed. He isn't a good choice for a beginner, since he frightens easily and takes a long time to get used to new experiences.

If a puppy scores mostly 6s, the dog is independent. He is not affectionate and may dislike petting and cuddling. It is difficult to establish a relationship with him whether he is a working dog or a companion. He is not recommended for children who may force attention on him; he is not a beginner's dog.

The tests are most accurate if done at seven weeks of age when there is no learned behavior yet, but are helpful at any age.

In the case of Gus, Mrs. Sanders' dog, he was obviously a number 1-type dog. He was very aggressive and dominant. He might have done very well with an experienced dog trainer—someone he respected—but not with someone like Mrs. Sanders, who thought it cruel to punish a dog for bad behavior, and who let Gus do what he wanted. Mrs. Sanders should have adopted a puppy with a type 3 personality. These puppies seem to train themselves and are generally submissive, so they wouldn't take advantage of the fact that their guardian had no leadership qualities.

The other mistake Mrs. Sanders made was interpreting Gus' body language in strictly human terms. She thought it was cute that Gus played so roughly with her; she thought he was just being a good watchdog when he growled at other people or animals around her. She reinforced and encouraged dominant behavior, interpreting it as protective or playful. She would have been shattered if Gus "protected" her from a visiting grandson or neighborhood child. She should have watched the *How Smart Is Your Puppy?* video and discussed the results with her veterinarian or obedience trainer to learn the appropriate training techniques for Gus.

We've all heard the expression concerning communication, "They weren't on the same wavelength." It's very important to match puppies to guardians who are on the same wavelength—so that they can readily communicate and interact and enjoy each other to the fullest.

Doing the tests on an adult dog you already have is also important. By discovering the strengths and weaknesses of your dog, you can see what areas need to be worked on, and you can utilize the services of a dog trainer to minimize problem areas and encourage positive traits. By getting dog and human closer to being on the same wavelength, the communication and bonding between them can flourish. ✿

## It's Best to
## Eat Crow While It's
## Still Warm

I walked into the exam room and saw that Mrs. Anderson had brought her black cat in for a large wound near its tail.

I poked around, then lifted the cat's tail and looked at his derriere to ascertain his sexual status. "It looks like Sammy got into a fight and has an abscess. Sammy was probably fighting because he's not neutered. Why don't you let me anesthetize him, treat the abscess, and neuter him at the same time?"

Mrs. Anderson glared at me. "What do you mean, he's not neutered?" she demanded.

I lifted the tail and pointed to the two rather large pieces of evidence.

Mrs. Anderson's face took on a crimson hue. Her eyes squinted, and her mouth pinched downward. "I brought him in last June and you *charged* me for neutering him. Now, you're telling me that you never neutered him—and he's sick and injured because of that?" she bellowed, leaning closer as if to strike.

I felt nauseous. I grabbed the record and backed up out of range as I read. Sure enough, Mrs. Anderson had brought Sammy in for neutering six months ago—and we had, in fact, charged her for doing it. I reached over and felt the two testicles—they weren't just scar tissue or fluffs of hair, they were the real McCoy.

Mrs. Anderson seemed to be hyperventilating and appeared ready to erupt. "Well?" she demanded, tapping her foot.

"Well—you're absolutely right! I couldn't be more sorry! I don't know how it could have happened, but somehow the procedure wasn't done, and you were charged and Sammy was sent home, because the receptionist thought the surgery had been completed. Again, please accept my apologies."

Mrs. Anderson wasn't soothed. "I caught you red-handed. You, in effect, stole from me—and lied too. And poor Sammy could have been killed in that fight—all because of you. He might even have kittens out there."

I thought of the pun, "There's a *vas deferens* between kittens and no kittens," but looking in Mrs. Anderson's eyes quickly erased the humor. "It was an honest, albeit stupid error, Mrs. Anderson. Someone must have erased it from the surgery schedule, thinking it done. But I'll personally do it myself this time, and..." I hastened to add, seeing her clench her jaw, "I'll treat the abscess and, of course, there'll be no charge." I tucked Sammy under my arm and quickly departed.

I did castrate Sammy and treat the abscess myself. Reluctantly, I called Mrs. Anderson to tell her that Sammy did just fine and was waking up. I stood by the phone for a full five minutes listening to her threats and verbal abuse. Having had time to think about it had refueled her anger and indignation. I meekly said, "You're absolutely right, Mrs. Anderson. But you can bet I'll bring this up at our next office meeting, and we'll devise some additional precautions to be sure this doesn't happen to anyone else in the future."

"Would looking to see if there were still testicles or not have been too much trouble for you or your staff?" she asked caustically.

"No, ma'am, it wouldn't. Again, I'm sorry. And you can pick Sammy up tomorrow morning. Goodbye!" I gave a loud exhale in relief at the end of the conversation and hurried to my next client.

The next day Mrs. Anderson picked Sammy up and reminded the receptionist that IT had BETTER be done THIS time!

About one hour after she and Sammy departed; the receptionist interrupted me to say that Mrs. Anderson was on the phone again, demanding to talk to me.

I dragged myself to the phone, trying to prepare myself for the conversation. "Hello, Mrs. Anderson? This is Dr. Pasten."

"Oh, hello, Dr. Laura." I looked into the phone receiver with disbelief. *This* Mrs. Anderson sounded sweet and friendly.

"I had to call you right away, Dr. Laura, and . . . and . . . apologize. You see . . . Sammy just came home. . . ."

Yes, you guessed it. Mrs. Anderson had seen a black cat on her front lawn and assumed it was Sammy. He didn't act quite right, but after all, he *was* sick. *That* black cat had not been neutered. While that cat was recuperating in her house, the real Sammy came home. She didn't know who the faux Sammy belonged to. She said he had been very vocal (probably saying, "Let meow 'ta here!"). I told her to quietly release the now-neutered stray black cat back into the neighborhood. Since then I've often wondered if the cat's owners ever noticed something was missing. . . .

There are many reasons to neuter a cat—decreasing the likelihood of spraying, roaming, breeding, and fighting are the most common ones.

Many people say they can smell urine in the house, but they have never seen their cat spray anything. A cat is probably spraying when he backs up to walls and twitches his tail or treads his hind feet. If you see him starting to back up and quiver his tail, call his name and interrupt him, or inhibit his spraying by pulling his tail down. Research has shown that cats don't spray on objects previously marked with facial pheromones or odors. Studies for a European product called Feliway show that within ten days of applying this simulated pheromone, cats decrease their spraying by 80 percent. Cornell University reported good results using Buspirone, an anxiety drug that reduced spraying by 75 percent. Many veterinarians use Elavil, and some use a product originally developed for birth control, but the best treatment is prevention, by neutering the cat.

∞ ∞ ∞

Did you hear about some of the experiments concerning neutering the dominant tomcat in a neighborhood? First, some background on cats. Cats are spontaneous ovulators—one reason they so readily get pregnant and have litters over and over again. Animals like dogs and humans have regular cycles—they ovulate, and if there is sex while the egg(s) are there, they can become pregnant. When cats mate, however, the stimulation of the penis causes the female to ovulate, thus assuring pregnancy.

There is also a definite "pecking" order of cats. The dominant male cat has first rights of breeding—only after he leaves the scene will other subservient males dare to breed. Most of us have heard the caterwauling of male cats as they fight for the privilege of being the dominant male.

Overpopulation of unwanted feral cats has always been a problem. Since the cats are wild, obviously no guardians can bring them in for neutering, and it is very expensive and time-consuming for animal control officers to hunt them down and capture them. So an experiment was tried. People staked out various neighborhoods with caged female cats. All night long researchers hid behind bushes and observed the cat fights to see who was regarded as the dominant male cat. Then they captured that male and vasectomized him! It was their hope that by vasectomizing the dominant male, he would breed most of the females, but he wouldn't impregnate them, thereby decreasing the feral cat population. Good idea, huh? I heard that it was quite successful at first, but since people and their animals are so mobile, new dominant male cats were regularly introduced into neighborhoods, thus negating their work. It also became increasingly difficult to get employees to do the night duty.

◈◈◈◈◈

Do you know why a male cat is called a tomcat? In 1760 an anonymous story was published, called "The Life and Adventures of a Cat." In it the "ram cat," as a male was then known, was given the name "Tom the Cat." The story enjoyed great popularity, and everyone started calling a male cat "Tom" rather than a "ram," and the word *tomcat* has been used now for over 200 years. ☀

# Stay Away from the South End of a Northbound Horse

eterinary medicine is a series of emergencies and dramas—tense, fatiguing, and, of course, rewarding. Stressful times lend themselves to black humor—I am not immune. I'll relate to you one of the blackest—and most enjoyable—stunts I've ever pulled on my husband.

I raised pure Polish Arabian Horses—beautiful and expensive. I say "I," because though we are married, my husband chose not to be involved—other than to pay the bills, of course. One of my most prized mares was due to be bred the second week of April; April Fools' Day was just around the corner. A wicked, but terribly fun, plan came to mind.

I told my husband that I had an important veterinary seminar to go to in a few days, and that the large animal veterinarian who usually helped me would be unavailable due to an endurance ride he was vetting. I told him that the mare might ovulate while I was gone, and he'd have to arrange to get her bred—otherwise, we'd miss breeding that month. The foal would therefore be born later in the year, which would make it less valuable in the show ring (it would be hard to compete with more mature horses).

He had a million reasons why he didn't want to get involved, but as is usually the way with husbands, he came around. I told him that she'd probably ovulate before I left, so not to worry. But, just in case, I'd show him what to do.

Have you ever seen a veterinarian checking to see if a horse has ovulated and is ready to be bred? She puts on a long glove that goes up to her shoulder. She lubricates the glove and inserts her entire hand and arm up the rectum of the horse. With her arm fully enveloped, her body right next to the horse's derriere, she feels the bottom of the horse's rectum for the fist-size masses that are the ovaries in the tissues below. Not something Gordon relished participating in.

I told him that there was a new product out. It was a device that changed color from increased body heat when the horse ovulated. If he'd have to check her, I'd insert this device in the rectum over the ovaries; he'd just have to retrieve it later in the day and see if it had turned a bright blue color, which meant she could be bred. Of course, you realize, there is *no* such device—and if one were to be invented, the horse would poop it out. But Gordon is a trusting soul—or at least he *was*.

Sure enough, the morning of my important seminar—it happened to be April 1, of course—I told him the bad news. He'd have to check the mare for ovulation. I arranged to have our neighbor come over to hold the horse for him. And with a look of total sympathy, I told him that I couldn't find my long examination glove—the one that would protect his arm. I apologized profusely and told him he'd have to use a pair of gloves that only went to the wrist—he'd just have to scrub up his "soiled" arm afterward. He whimpered and then roared, demanding to know why we couldn't just call another veterinarian. I patiently reminded him that this mare was very nervous and wouldn't tolerate the procedure from anyone she didn't know. I told him I'd inserted the device and reminded him how important it was to see if it had turned blue. I left him grumbling and griping.

Periodically, I'd burst out laughing all day long—the image of my CEO husband doing a rectal palpation with a short glove and looking for an imaginary device was just too funny. My neighbor tells the story:

"I came over to help Laura play this April Fools' joke on Gordon. I told him she'd asked me to hold the horse for him. He clearly looked upset, said a few expletives, but stomped to the barn to get the mare.

I held the mare by her halter as he put on these tiny gloves that didn't even come to his wrist. He put the lubricant on and gingerly inserted his hand into the rectum. The horse promptly farted, causing Gordon to turn a shade of green. He kept inching his hand up the rectum until his whole arm was inside. You could see him rotating his arm and hand in all directions, trying to find the device which was supposed to be there. After awhile, totally flustered, he raged, 'Damn, I can't find the f____ng thing! What should I do?'

I took out my camera and took a picture of him with his arm up the horse's behind, then pulled out a piece of paper. 'Your wife told me to read this to you if you had trouble finding the device.'

'Well, now you tell me! Read the damn thing!' he yelled.

I opened up the paper and showed it to him. It merely said, 'April Fools'!' "

⁊⁊⁊⁊⁊⁊

Talking about pranks, do you know why we use the expression, "He let the cat out of the bag"? Desmond Morris tells us in *Illustrated Cat Watching* that the origin of this phrase, meaning "He gave away a secret," dates back to the eighteenth century, when it referred to a market-day trick. Piglets were often taken to market in a small sack, or bag, to be sold. The trickster would put a cat in a bag and pretend that it was a pig. If the buyer insisted on seeing it, he would be told that it was too lively to risk opening up the bag, as the animal might escape. If the cat struggled so much that the trickster let the cat out of the bag, his secret was exposed. A popular name for the bag itself was a "poke," hence that other expression "Never buy a pig in a poke."

Some people, including my husband, thought my playful behavior with my April Fools' joke was a bit cruel (I, of course, disagree). And some people think that a cat that plays with its prey is cruel. Horrified humans have often experienced the shock of finding their cat torturing a small bird or mouse. The cat indulges in a cruel game of either hit-and-chase or trap-and-release—the poor petrified victim may actually die of

**57**

shock before the final coup de grâce can be delivered. Why does the cat do it? Behaviorist Desmond Morris explains that this "toying with food" is not the behavior of a wild cat.

Playing with prey is the behavior of a well-fed companion animal, which has been starved of hunting activity and can't bear to end the chase, prolonging it as much as possible until the prey dies. Wild cats, dependent on the prey for food, can't take the risk of the prey getting away, so they kill it quickly—with two exceptions:

Female cats have to bring live prey back to the nest to demonstrate killing to their kittens. And cats also delay killing their prey if they are nervous about the prey's ability to defend itself. When a feral cat attacks a large rat, he knows that the rat can give him a nasty bite, so the cat subdues it before attempting to make the killing-bite. The cat swings a lightning blow with its claws extended. In quick succession it may beat a rat this way and that until it is dazed and dizzy. Only then does the cat risk going in close with its face for the killing-bite.

Do you know why a kitten sometimes throws a toy into the air when playing? Again, Desmond Morris knows the answer. We've all seen a kitten flip one of its paws under a ball, flinging the ball up into the air and backward over its head. As the ball flies through the air, the kitten swings around and follows it, pouncing on it and "killing it" yet again. The usual interpretation of this playful behavior is that the kitten is being inventive and playful, but that is not the whole story.

In the wild state, cats have three different patterns of attack, depending on whether they are hunting mice, birds, or fish. With mice, they stalk, pounce, trap with the front feet, and then bite. With birds they stalk, pounce, and then, if the bird flies up into the air, they leap up after it, swiping at with both front feet at once. If they are quick enough and trap the bird's body in the pincher movement of their front legs, they pull it down to the ground for the killing-bite.

Less familiar is the way in which cats hunt for fish. They do this by lying in wait at the water's edge and then, when an unwary fish swims near, they dip a paw swiftly into the water and slide it rapidly under the fish's body, flipping the fish up out of the water. The direction of the flip is back and over the cat's shoulders, and it flips the fish clear of the water. As the startled fish lands on the grass behind the cat, the hunter swings around and pounces.

Recognize the behavior in your kitten? It is these instinctive fishing actions that you have seen when your kitten flips things in the air. A Dutch research project was able to reveal that the scooping up of fish from the water, using the "flip-up" action, develops early and without the benefit of maternal instruction. Kittens that are allowed to hunt fish regularly from their fifth week of life onward, but in the absence of their mother, became successful anglers by the age of seven weeks. So the playful kitten throwing a ball over its shoulder is really doing no more than it would do for real if it were growing up in the wild, near a pond or river.

In most species of mammals, playfulness fades as individuals become adults. Two notable exceptions to this rule are dogs and people. In *Illustrated Dogwatching,* Desmond Morris explains that during the course of evolution humans became "juvenile apes," retaining our childhood curiosity and our playfulness right through our adult lives. This gave us our remarkable inventiveness (as in my April Fools' joke).

Just as we are juvenile apes, so dogs are juvenile wolves. As adults, all breeds of domestic dogs remain unusually playful. One of the problems they have to face is how to indicate to other dogs, or to people, that they are in a playful mood. Since play often involves mock fighting and mock fleeing, it is crucial to make it clear that a particular action is only in fun and is not to be taken seriously. This is done by performing special play-invitation displays. Learning to read these signals is one aspect of communicating with your companion animal.

The most popular of these signals is the play-bow, in which the dog dramatically lowers the front half of its body while keeping its rear end raised. If the companion responds, there follows either a play-chase or a play-fight. In origin, it has been suggested that the play-bow is a modified stretching movement similar to the kind of leg-stretching that is seen when a dog wakes up. By making a "stretch" display, the animal indicates that is relaxed and that the attacking and fleeing that are about to start are therefore not serious.

There is also the play-face, an expression that is the canine equivalent of the human smile. The expression is the opposite of the snarl of an angry dog—it shows that the dog is completely nonaggressive in its play. Other incitements to join in play include nudging, pawing, and offering a ball or stick. Nudging and pawing are infantile feeding behaviors.

For dogs to play well as adults it is crucial that they play with littermates when young. It is during the first few months of life that puppies discover the need to perform what is called the "soft-bite." At first, when they start wrestling with one another their sharp teeth cause yelps and whines of pain. But they quickly realize that hard biting stops the playful rough-and-tumble, and they learn to inhibit the strength of their jaw movements. Dogs that have been isolated when young and deprived of this puppy play-phase sometimes become troublemakers as adults. Lacking the soft-bite, they hurt their playmates, and real fighting may erupt. Such dogs become pests in public parks where dogs gather to play.

So, think of some playful pranks of your own. Remember Herbert Spencer's words: "We don't stop playing because we grow old, we grow old because we stop playing." ✸

# When God Measures Man, He Puts the Tape around the Heart, Not the Head

A fellow veterinarian and friend of mine died a year ago from a brain tumor. As his friends gathered around his grave for the service, snatches of conversation could be heard. "Hard to believe. . . ." "Just two months since the diagnosis. . . ." "So young. . . ." Everyone was trying to come to grips with the fact that one of the best healers we knew was lying, cold and still, within the ground.

I felt numb—the service was a blur, but finally it appeared to be over. Friends and family hugged and clung to each other, an attempt to mitigate the grief. Some people started drifting toward their cars, purposefully, it appeared, measuring their steps lest they appear too anxious to leave.

All movements and murmurs stopped when a strange, eerie sound was heard from the open grave. Eyes darted from face to face seeking answers. Van's wife gave a nervous chuckle and said, "Don't worry, it's just his beeper!"

The thought of his wife choosing to include his beeper in the coffin, and the imagery of this poor beleaguered doctor even now being paged from beyond rather than resting in peace made us all smile and realize that his work day was just beginning, not ending.

≈ ⊗ ⊗ ⊗ ⊗

Death is the hardest part of veterinary medicine; sometimes you put your heart and soul into saving a patient, only to have her take her last spasms of breath while you are praying to God to save her. And, for me, the worst of all—when you have to hasten her death throes and lessen her agony with a lethal injection. Playing God and ending her life, even as she continues to struggle to survive.

Each and every patient that I have had to put to sleep has weighed heavy on my soul—a leaden ghost of guilt and sadness to heap upon my shoulders. But two such deaths replay over and over and over again in my mind.

The first happened many years ago, only a few months after I completed my internship. I have mentally replayed the event so often that every detail remains vivid. I was working for another veterinarian. It was his belief that if a guardian wanted an animal put to sleep, we did it, period. He believed that if we didn't, the guardian would take the animal to a shelter where they would end the animal's life much less humanely.

It was a crisp autumn day, with each slight breeze carrying a few red and golden maple leaves to the ground. A man brought in a black and white Border Collie mix and said we were to euthanize (humanely put to sleep) his dog—the guardian was being transferred; he couldn't take

**65**

his dog, and he couldn't bear the thought of his dog being abused by someone or sitting on death row at the animal shelter. Since I was a new employee, it was my job to put Sadie to sleep.

I loaded my syringe with the "pink juice," petted this lovely dog and told her I was sorry, and proceeded. She slowly wagged her tail, and trustingly licked my hand as I pushed in the remaining fluid while her body crumpled. It seemed like I had violated every oath I made to God or to my profession—it was a sin, even though I would have been fired had I refused to do it. Even now, many years later, I would do anything to undo that act, but, of course, I can't—it remains a scar on my heart and my honor.

I vowed never again to euthanize any animal unless it was suffering and couldn't be saved, and when that became an issue with my employer, I mustered the gumption and national debt-sized loan to open my own hospital where I could make the rules. I have been fortunate to make a difference in some people and animals' lives, but my hand still feels the cosmic guilt tattooed by Sadie's gentle lick.

The second euthanasia forever to haunt me was putting my sixteen-year-old Standard Schnauzer, Tybo, to sleep. Tybo had a malignant cancer that had metastasized to his spine, causing him excruciating pain and an inability to walk without assistance. Tybo had been happy and healthy until "the last week from Hell," when the cancer ravaged his spinal cord. I fought to get the tumor in remission to give us a little more time together, a few more butterflies for him to chase, a few more table scraps for him to savor. But the cancer was stronger than all my training and all my prayers, and I finally had to end his suffering. He had always been there for me during his life; I would be there for him in his death.

I drew up the euthanasia solution into the syringe and set it next to me on the floor. I murmured things to Tybo as I stroked him—told him what a gallant dog he was, how handsome, how loving, how clever—that he was the best friend I'd ever had. I recounted special moments like when we were hiking together in the Desolation Wilderness area, and he disappeared in pursuit of some creature. As I trekked up the mountain, I called his name repeatedly. Then I saw a distant speck on the other side of a very large ice-cold lake, saw the speck enter the freezing waters and gallantly swim toward my calls. He'd never been a good swimmer—his enthusiasm made him swim upright, somewhat like a person treading water—but he faithfully responded to my command and made his numb legs continue to thrash, bringing him closer and closer. I watched in quiet horror, certain the frigid waters would claim my pal, but the speck kept getting larger and larger as he drew closer. I half-ran, half-stumbled down the mountain, wading into the water to receive my loyal friend who was violently shaking from hypothermia. He'd sooner have died than let me down—such was the magnitude of his heart.

What is this rapport between dogs and humans, so strong that it surpasses the natural instinct for survival? Again and again one sees that a dog accepts a human being as master or mistress, thereafter subordinating his instinct for survival to his sense of duty and devotion. And so it was with Tybo.

I kissed the top of his head, nuzzled in his beard, and whispered in his ear that I loved him and that he'd always be "my little guy." Through blinding tears I managed to depress the plunger, pushing the solution into his veins. At first he was stoic—after all, I was always injecting one thing or another these days—and then as it started to take effect, he gave me a startled look. That look still haunts me. Why had he been startled? Was he certain I'd never harm him? Had I violated his trust? Then Tybo sighed and collapsed in my arms. It was over—his life-force was gone— his eyes already dull and staring. He made one giant heave as if trying to regain life, then lay still. I stroked him harder and harder with each deluge of tears, telling him how sorry I was. The pain in my chest expanded into a massive, leaden ball; I felt like I couldn't breathe—not enough air and no will to live. At that moment, all that was good in my life was gone, snuffed out by my own two hands.

❧ ❧ ❧ ❧

In dealing with the death of an animal, I gain some comfort from an anonymous story called "The Rainbow Bridge" that a client once gave me:

There is a bridge connecting Heaven and Earth. It is called "the

Rainbow Bridge" because of its many colors. Just this side of the Rainbow Bridge there is a land of meadows, hills, and valleys with lush green grass.

When a beloved animal dies, the animal goes to this place. There is always food and water and warm spring weather. The old and frail animals are young again. Those who were maimed are made whole again. They play all day with each other.

There is only one thing missing. They are not with the special person who loved them on Earth. So each day they run and play until the day comes when one of them suddenly stops playing and looks up. The nose twitches. The ears are up. The eyes are staring. And that one suddenly runs from the group.

You have been seen, and when you and your special friend meet, you take him or her in your arms and embrace. Your face is kissed again and again and again, and you look once more into the eyes of your trusting companion.

Then you cross the Rainbow Bridge together, never again to be separated. ☀

# The Doctor Has
# "Inside" Information

As I felt the Doberman Pinscher's abdomen, the pathetic little puppy reacted with spasms of vomiting. The man looked at me, his face full of reproach. I explained that I was feeling the dog's tummy to see if it were painful, since so many puppies ingest foreign objects.

The man made a snorting sound. "This is a purebred dog, not some damn mongrel. I feed him nothing but the best food. He isn't starving—he doesn't eat junk. We constantly watch him—that's just not possible."

I reviewed my notes. Duke was lethargic, not eating, and had diarrhea. I added a notation about abdominal tenderness. "I really think we should take an abdominal X ray in case Duke accidentally ingested something he shouldn't have."

"You doctors are always finding ways to jack up the bill. I told you he didn't get into anything!" stormed the man.

"Well, let's start with a blood panel—see if we can get any clues from that." I looked at the client for his reaction.

He sighed at the inevitable and glared into my eyes.

I had the definite impression he wanted me to know that he was onto my scam—unnecessary lab work to increase the bill. I smiled as if all was well. "How about I keep Duke one night for observation? That way we can watch him for any further problems while we wait for the test results."

"Humph! I knew you'd find a way—you doctors! But, okay. We spent a lot of money on this dog and don't want to lose it. Call me the moment you finally know something—and don't be telling me about a bunch of fancy tests you want to do."

I sent in the lab work, requesting immediate results. In a few hours I heard the whir of the fax machine—Duke's results. He was anemic—definitely something I hadn't expected. I got Duke out for further examination. This time when I looked at his gums, I saw little hemorrhages or bruises. Things were getting more serious. I felt his abdomen again; he yelped. I stared at the wretched pup as I pondered all the possible diagnoses.

I saw one of the technicians looking at me. "Let's get abdominal X rays," I said.

"But I thought the owner wouldn't okay the expense of X rays?"

"I know, but I really have to rule out ingestion of a foreign body; I couldn't live with myself if he died, and I could have prevented it. If we find something, I'll tell him. If we don't find anything, no charge. . . . It'll be our secret."

"You doctors—you're all alike—giving away the store," she said over her shoulder as she walked toward the X-ray room with Duke.

The technician came back, a broad smile on her face. "Your X rays are ready, doctor."

I put the still-wet films on the viewer. They showed three densities in the stomach—small, round things. "That's it! Pennies! A zinc toxicity!"

"Pennies? I thought they were made of copper," she said.

"Prior to 1983, they were, but since then they are 99 percent zinc. And zinc toxicity causes hemolytic anemia and all of Duke's symptoms. That's it! Now, all we have to do is convince Mr. 'I know you're out for the money' to let me do surgery."

I called Duke's guardian and explained that I had taken the X rays, planning to absorb the cost if they revealed nothing, but in fact they showed three foreign objects that I believed to be pennies.

There was a long pause. "How do I know that X ray is of my dog, or that you didn't just put three coins on top of Duke when you took the X ray to make it look like they were in his stomach?

I tried to keep my tone even. "You'll just have to trust me, I'm afraid. Can I do the surgery? He should have it right away."

There was a lot of grumbling and expletives, but he finally agreed.

Duke was anesthetized and prepped for surgery. I opened the stomach, and there were the three pennies just as we thought. I looked at their dates—one was dated 1982, one was dated 1979, and one was dated 1980. These pennies were made prior to 1983—they had to be copper, which didn't fit with the lab work! I probed the stomach with my gloved finger, reaching deep into the pyloric region. "Aha! Another penny! And the date . . . 1986! The culprit! Two pennies must have been stuck together when the X ray was taken, making it look like three rather than four pennies!" I removed the offending zinc penny and sewed Duke back up.

Duke recovered nicely. As the man paid the bill, he grumbled something about how he should have just tried Pepto Bismol. "And what about my four pennies?" he demanded.

"Pardon me?" I said.

"Where's the four pennies you took out of Duke?"

I gave him the four pennies plus an additional one. "Keep the change," I replied.

⟨ೋ ೨೯ೕ ೨೯ೕ ೨೯⟩

I remember telling my technician that I'd *never* get another case like that of zinc toxicity again.

Not one week later, a woman came in with two children and a Miniature Schnauzer. The kids were punching and shoving each other, one accusing the other of some misdeed, and the other protesting loudly.

Over the din, Missy's guardians said the Schnauzer had had a poor appetite and diarrhea for a week. I examined Missy. She was a pretty, silver girl with a long flowing beard and expressive brown eyes. But her eyes were filled with pain. Her mucous membranes were pale; she was breathing rapidly, and her temperature was 103 degrees.

"Did so."

"Did not."

"You took it. Admit it!"

"Did not."

"Tommy, Cindy . . . stop it! The doctor needs to think!"

"But Mom . . . Tommy took my favorite Monopoly piece—you know the little hat. Make him give it back!"

"I said stop it! We'll talk about it when we get home," the mother said in a menacing tone.

"That could do it," I said softly to myself. "When did your Monopoly piece disappear?"

The kids and mother looked at me as if I just made wind.

"When did the hat disappear?" I asked again.

The girl looked at me suspiciously, but muttered, "A week or so ago. I know Tommy took it—he was playing with it. I told him to put it down." She stuck her tongue out at him.

"Did not!" He eyed her angrily.

The mother started to swat them both.

"Wait! That could be it. Missy could have swallowed the Monopoly hat piece. I remember reading that they are made of zinc—which could cause her symptoms. Let's take an X ray and see."

## The Doctor Has "Inside" Information

Well, you know the rest of the story. The X ray showed a little hat-shaped item. Tommy looked quite smug. Missy did well in surgery, though she's been banned from the room when they play Monopoly now. ✿

**I Said, Give Your Dog a Bone, Not a Ph___**

I heard an interesting story on the news. A woman purchased a cellular phone for her roommate for Christmas. Her friend opened the present, called the phone company to activate it, then placed it under the Christmas tree with the other gifts. Later, the woman wanted to use the phone but couldn't find it. Thinking she had misplaced it, she had the brilliant idea of dialing the phone number and listening for its ring.

Imagine her shock when she heard the faint sounds of a phone ringing right next to her—from the inside of her dog!

You guessed it! These newfangled phones are so darn compact now; it had the mistress' scent on it; and it was fun to play with—too much temptation for ol' Snoopy, the bloodhound.

She took Snoopy to the veterinarian, and X rays confirmed it. The phone was in his stomach. Well, two weeks' salary and a surgery later, Snoopy was fine. The phone still worked, by the way, but Snoopy doesn't touch it—doesn't have the stomach for it!

෧ ෧෧ ෧෧ ෧

Dogs and cats eat the darnedest things. Often a cat will repeatedly make choking sounds. The human keeps dosing him with hairball medicine, only to find out that a swallowed thread is wrapped around the base of his tongue and down his throat. I have removed diapers, feminine hygiene products, balls, and even a watch from the stomachs of dogs. (I know, I know. *Time* for surgery or *time* passes, right?) Animals will eat just about anything, so it's up to us to make smart choices about items they are exposed to, as well as what food to give them.

All animal guardians should read Dr. Richard Pitcairn's and Susan Pitcairn's book, *Dr. Pitcairn's Complete Guide to Natural Health for Dogs and Cats.* These writers have done their homework about commercial animal foods, and the results are startling.

They found that even premium pet foods contain slaughterhouse wastes, toxic products from spoiled foodstuffs, non-nutritive fillers, heavy-metal contaminants, pesticides, herbicides, drug residues, and artificial colors, flavors, and preservatives.

Meat contains much more pesticide residue, heavy metals, and other toxic pollutants than food from plant sources. Contamination with lead, for example, can be very severe. In one study, a sampling of canned pet foods revealed levels ranging from 0.9 to 7.00 parts per million (ppm) in cat foods and 1.0 to 5.6 ppm in dog foods. Daily intake of only six ounces of such foods could exceed the dose of lead considered potentially toxic for children. The Pitcairns maintain that much of this contamination comes from using bone meal in animal foods. Though it is an excellent source of calcium and other minerals, the bones of American cattle contain high levels of lead from the long-term use of leaded gasoline in automobiles in their environment.

In *The Nontoxic Home and Office,* author Deborah Lynn Dadd writes: "Each year about 116,000 mammals and nearly 15 million birds are condemned for use for human consumption 'before' slaughter. After killing, another 325,000 carcasses are discarded and more than 5.5 million major parts are cut away because they are determined to be diseased. Shockingly, 140,000 tons of poultry are condemned annually, mainly from cancer. All these diseased animals, cancers, and discarded parts than cannot be sold or processed into human food, is made into . . . ANIMAL FEED." yes, food for your companion animals—in the form of dry, canned, or semimoist pet food.

Not only that, but many veterinarians don't pay to have their dead animals buried; pick-up service is provided free in exchange for the carcasses to be used for animal food. Imagine, someone's dog or cat might be eating someone else's beloved companion—or worse yet, a recently departed member of their own family. Be sure and specify to your veterinarian that you want your animal to be buried or cremated—not used for pet food.

I really have a problem using animals with cancer for pet food. We now know that many cancers are caused by viruses (but they also need host genes to replicate). Viruses aren't killed by normal heating and processing of foods—so using animals with cancer (which possibly contain these viruses) for feed could be giving our animals cancer!

The Pitcairns report that in all but two or three states, the law allows pet food makers to use what are called 4-D sources—that is, tissues from animals that are dead, dying, disabled, or diseased when they arrive at the slaughterhouse. Other pet food ingredients include food rejected by the USDA for human consumption, such as moldy grains or rancid animal fats. Manufacturers can, however, voluntarily submit to continuous government inspection of their products' ingredients and their plant facilities. Such products bear a label saying that the USDA has packed them under continuous inspection.

What can you do, besides write to your congresspeople to change these laws? Ask your veterinarian for recipes for homemade animal food. Make a big batch and freeze it, thawing it as needed. Regarding commercial foods, remember the adage, "You get what you pay for." The current commercial food that I feed my dogs is Wysong. Its main ingredient (always the first thing listed in the ingredients) is chicken—not byproducts or corn like so many; it has no non-nutritional additives; it includes active enzymes added after processing and has special oxygen barrier packaging to preserve nutrients.

Seeing what's in so many commercial animal foods, no wonder dogs say, "Barf! Barf!" ☀

# Hiss and Make Up

 ike many hospitals, mine has three exam rooms in tandem, with a door on each side—one for the client and one for the doctor. One day, I was told there was a boa constrictor in Exam Room 3. As I walked past Exam Room 1, I saw a person holding the tail end of a snake; as I walked past Exam Room 2, another person held part of the snake; and as I walked into Exam Room 3, two people held the front end of that snake. We're talking a *big* snake.

This twelve-foot Boa Constrictor was named Caesar, and he had a big bump on his forehead. I thought it was an abscess (snakes form "cottage cheese"-type abscesses, not the fluid type that mammals get) or possibly a tumor, and an excision biopsy (removal of all involved tissues and subsequent testing) would fix him up. After hearing the risks of anesthesia on large snakes, the guardian refused it. I forcefully had to hold down this writhing snake and cut into it with no anesthesia, or they were not going to let me treat him.

Holding my scalpel more like a dagger or ice pick than an instrument, I dug through the thick skin and scales to remove the hard mass, using great pressure and strength to remove the stubborn tissue. The mass I removed proved to be an abscess, and I sewed our scaly friend back together—again, having to use great force to get the needle to penetrate the scales.

After the surgery, looking pleased, the guardian casually said, "Well, that certainly went better than at the other vet's." He hadn't told me the snake had been to another vet. . . .

"What do you mean?" I queried apprehensively.

"We took him to another hospital last week. The vet didn't change his smock before he came in, so my snake must have smelled blood. He bit the doctor's neck, wrapped around him, knocked the vet to the ground, and proceeded to constrict. We tried to unwind Caesar but couldn't get his head and teeth loose from the vet's throat, nor could we find the snake's tail; he had buried it under his body. We had nothing to pull on to unwind him."

I gulped. "So what happened?"

"The vet's head turned kinda blackish. We yelled for help, and another vet put some acid from the lab into Caesar's nostrils. He finally let go so we could unwind him. The doctor had to go to a hospital in an ambulance!"

"Is he okay?" I asked, trying not to reveal my anger at the client for "forgetting" to mention this little story before I did my brutal surgery.

"The receptionist said his neck was black and blue, and he had draining abscesses from the bite, but he was okay. He should have known

**87**

better than to come into the room with a dirty smock—right?"

I hadn't changed smocks before coming into the room either. How many veterinarians change smocks twenty times a day? But now I have to agree that maybe changing uniforms before seeing a snake is a good idea. Curtly, I told the man that keeping a boa over six feet long was illegal, and that if he came back again, I really would have to report him.

☙ ❧☙ ❧☙ ❧

Like Caesar, our snake friend, cats commonly get abscesses—usually from getting bitten by another cat. Cats' teeth are needle-like and sharp; they have a great amount of bacteria on them. So when a cat bites another cat, bacteria are deposited under the skin; it's such a small wound that the skin heals rapidly, trapping the bacteria and debris under the skin to cause an abscess. Approximately 50 percent of all cat bites will become abscessed (you will usually notice it approximately three days after the bite).

Cats will usually get abscesses around the head and front legs or at the base of the tail. Wounds around the head indicate that your cat was either the aggressor or was at least fighting back. Wounds around the tail area or on the rear legs mean that your cat was trying to get away.

After being scratched or bitten by a cat, some people will develop a fever, malaise, and large lymph nodes near the scratch or bite. These symptoms usually occur one to two weeks after the injury, and the syndrome is called Cat Scratch Fever. If you develop any of these problems, see your doctor—usually antibiotics will fix you right up.

A cat will usually bite or scratch you only when it feels threatened. So let's discuss some techniques for communicating your benign intentions toward cats.

While the cat is looking at you, gradually sit down on your heels. When a cat is threatened, he raises himself as high as possible, so this submissive posture of yours will reassure him.

Now look away from the cat before allowing your gaze to return to his face. As you do so, half-close your eyes prior to restoring eye contact. Then, when you are looking at one another, blink several times. This is a reassuring signal used between cats that will also work between people and cats.

Once the cat gives you a signal that he has accepted you, get on even better terms by head-rubbing. Place your forehead against his, and rub your nose and chin against his head. This is a warm and affectionate greeting message often used between two friendly cats, so he'll get the message that you're signaling friendship.

Practice noticing the size of your cat's pupils. See how large and round her pupils are when she is stressed or fearful. Note how thin and slit-like they are when she is angry and feeling aggressive. Pay attention to your cat's body language; it speaks volumes. A cat's ears and tail are especially expressive.

When you are *talking* to your cat, simplify your thinking and look at the situation through your cat's point of view. Cats perceive our thoughts through mental images, senses (seeing, hearing, tasting, feeling, and smelling), and emotions. Cats are very emotionally oriented, so pay special attention to broadcasting emotions to your cat. A typical way of telling your cat good-bye when you go to work might look like this:

"Clyde, we'll see-touch each other when it's dark. Hold a mental picture of you petting and head-butting Clyde, and Clyde rubbing on your legs with love and gladness. Put a dark window in the background to give a time reference.

If you're leaving your cat for a number of days with a neighbor coming over daily to check on Clyde and feed him, visualize in the same manner. Imagine the neighbor coming over in the morning and evening (bright sun out and neighbor setting food dish down; dark outside and neighbor setting food dish down); repeat this for every day that you will be gone; that is, day, night; day, night; day, night, and so on, for the number of days until you return. Then visualize greeting Clyde with love and gladness, petting him, and Clyde rubbing on your legs, with a dark window in the background for a time reference. In this way, Clyde will know exactly what to expect and will be less likely to roam or suffer separation anxiety. ✸

# Opportunities Knock;
# Emergencies Ring

The ringing jarred me awake. 3:30 in the morning. Must be trouble! "This is Mel Jacobs. You gotta come right away, Doc. It's Beau. He's got that there rabies."

"Rabies? You sure? Isn't he vaccinated? What are the symptoms?" I was now thoroughly awake.

"Naw—meant to though. Damn shame! Best damn dog I ever had. Aah, he's, you know, drooling, circling, won't touch his water. . . ."

"Hydrophobic? Well, it does sound. . . ."

"Can ya come now? Hate to see 'im suffer-ol' Beau. Too risky trying to bring 'im in and all."

"I'll leave right now. See you in around fifteen minutes." I grabbed the rabies pole (a long pole with a slip noose at the end—a way to catch a rabid dog and keep him at arm's length) and euthanasia solution. Looking down at the ever-present little nicks and scratches on my hands, I made a mental note to wear rubber gloves while working with Beau.

As I drove toward Mel's ranch, anger welled. A damn fine dog, he said. Why didn't he give a damn fine rabies vaccine to him? He should be held responsible for Beau's having to be put to sleep. Should have to go to jail for second-degree murder or something.

I drove through the archway to Mel's property, noticing that all the lights seemed to be on in the house and barn with floodlights on all around his ranch. Mel was stooped over, nervously pacing in front of the house, shotgun slung over one arm.

I grabbed my rabies pole and bag. "What's the rifle for?"

"Case he attacks me, you know. Damn shame it is. Make it quick, Doc. He ain't ought to suffer." He jerked his chin in the direction of the barn.

Following his gaze, I saw Beau, a well-muscled Rottweiler. Sure enough, he looked demented, circling and waving his head about erratically, big strings of saliva dripping out of his mouth. Every few moments, he'd run to his water bowl, look like he'd want to drink, then back off.

"Looks like he's holding his mouth kind of funny," I said.

Mel nodded. "Lockjaw if I ever seen it."

I remembered a veterinary professor once saying that for most diagnoses, all that is needed is an ounce of knowledge, an ounce of intelligence, and a pound of thoroughness. There is no treatment for rabies, so I certainly didn't want to euthanize Beau if I didn't have to. I put on a pair of gloves and called Beau.

Mel backed up. "You ought not to be touching him—might bite ya—then where'll ya be?"

Beau obediently padded over. I opened his mouth, folding his upper lips over his teeth to prevent him from biting me. There was the culprit- a large bone lodged across his inner mouth between the teeth.

"Give him a pork chop bone recently?"

"Yeah, supposin' I did," he said suspiciously.

I pulled out the bone and held it up for inspection.

"Well, I'll be durn," Mel said, eyes bugging.

"Yeah, I'll be darn. Let's give this damn fine dog a rabies vaccine. What do you say?"

"Guess so." He licked his lips. "You're not going to charge me for a house call just to give a damn rabies shot are ya? I ain't some rich city folk, ya know."

I just smiled and said, "Some of us can learn by other people's mistakes. The rest of us have to be the 'other' people."

೧ ೨ ೧ ೨ ೧ ೨

This story had a happy ending, but it could have been a tragedy— Beau could have had rabies. He should have been vaccinated (and he shouldn't have been given a pork chop bone). But the recommendations for the frequency of vaccines as well as which vaccines to give is changing rapidly.

Everyone agrees about the importance of giving vaccines to prevent disease. But controversy is mounting over the potential dangers of vaccines for our companion animals; this same debate is raging over human vaccines.

Almost all vaccines, whether for people or animals, utilize cow serum in their production. In one vaccine, we therefore inject hundreds of foreign proteins from the cow serum. It's believed that reactions to these foreign proteins are responsible for many of the autoimmune diseases we are seeing today, such as like rheumatoid arthritis, diabetes, and certain thyroid problems.

In addition, blood from the same species of animal is involved in a vaccine; that is, dog serum for dog vaccines, human serum for human vaccines. Blood from as many as 200 donors could be involved in serum for a single vaccine. That's equivalent to using contaminated hypodermic needles from a couple hundred people. We all know about the hemophiliacs infected with HIV before we knew of its existence and how to test for it. And now it's believed that many cancers probably have a virus component (but, of course, there must be particular genes in the host to allow it to be activated in the body). Could we be introducing cancer-causing agents in vaccines? What are we exposing our animals and ourselves to by getting repeated vaccines?

What about flu vaccines? How smart is it to have unknown viruses and proteins from blood donors pumped into our bodies just to avoid being sick with the flu a few days? I believe that unless you're over sixty-five or are immune deficient, it would be wise to skip the flu vaccine.

Much research is being done on the dangers of vaccination. Studies in Europe, Asia, and Australia show that the DPT vaccine is a likely cause of crib death (SIDS, or Sudden Infant Death Syndrome) and asthma. Many researchers warn that we'll see an increase in illnesses that barely existed before mass vaccination programs.

Perhaps we shouldn't vaccinate for relatively harmless childhood diseases in animals or people. It's now believed that these diseases might be needed to build the immune system to fight off other things. In human cancer victims, for example, there has been a concerted effort to look through people's histories to see if cancer victims share some common history that could raise a red flag. The startling thing they had in common was that the patients listed surprisingly few childhood diseases, but had thorough vaccination regimens.

So the problems concerning vaccines are fourfold:

1. You might get the disease you are vaccinating for from residual virulence.

2. You might get a disease from contaminants.

3. You might develop an autoimmune reaction or disease.

4. You might need to contract some diseases to strengthen your immune system in early years.

So, what do I recommend? Only getting vaccines for diseases your animal is likely to become exposed to and only for diseases that are fatal, to justify the risk. I also recommend getting them as infrequently as possible while still maintaining a level of protection. Your veterinarian can now order from the laboratory serum titer tests for the various diseases that are covered by vaccines. In that way you can determine how long a particular vaccine lasts in your dog or cat (it varies greatly), and only vaccinate when your animal is no longer protected. Many people feel that a dog or cat over the age of ten should not receive any more vaccines (there's a greater chance of her having chronic problems that will be exasperated, and a greater chance that she still has an immunity to the disease in question).

But if you elect not to test to see if your animal still has sufficient antibodies to prevent disease, here are some general guidelines. In dogs, this would mean getting rabies vaccines every three years, parvo and Lyme disease vaccines every year to year and a half, and distemper every several years. For a cat I recommend distemper, leukemia, and rabies vaccines every three years. These recommendations are one-half to one-third as often as I recommended just six months ago—as I said, everyone is changing their protocols as more information is coming out on the subject.

Vaccinations are a good source of income for vets; there is much controversy and reluctance to change "old ways of thinking" and doctors are afraid of their liability for not making traditional vaccine recommendations. So it will be up to you to do your own research on this subject and tell us veterinarians what is right for you or your companion animals. ☀

# A Rubber Band,
# Like a Ring,
# Cuts Off Circulation

He's dying." The voice on the other end of the phone was barely a whisper; I strained to hear her. "You have an animal that's dying?" I said.

"Yes. A Collie—twelve years old. He's just lying there, doesn't eat, doesn't drink, doesn't even get up to go to the bathroom anymore. Can I pick up something to end his misery?"

"Has your dog been to a veterinarian for this problem? Can you bring him in, so I can see if there is anything I can do?"

"No, I vowed I wouldn't do that. I had a doxie—Fritz—that I took to the vet when he was dying. They poked, prodded, stuck him with a million needles and IVs, and Fritz died a slow, painful death, away from his home and those he loved. I vowed I wouldn't put another animal through that. It's obvious he's dying—I just need something to . . . you know, an overdose of sleeping pills or something."

"I'm afraid I can't give you anything that could be used to harm yourself or others—it's illegal. Couldn't you just bring in your dog—what's his name? And I could gently examine him and see if I could help? If there's nothing I can do without a lot of heroics, I could put him to sleep for you if it looks like he's suffering."

"His name's Buddy. I'm sorry; I know you're trying to help. But I really don't want to bring him in. Can you at least suggest something to make him feel better until he dies?"

This was a tough one. Not having any idea what was wrong with Buddy, what could I recommend that wouldn't hurt him and yet might help? I thought of Linda Tellington-Jones and her T-touch technique. "Have you heard of T-touch?" I asked.

"Yes, I think so—a sort of massage?"

"Kind of, although massage is done with the intent of affecting the muscular system, and T-touch reorganizes the nervous system and activates the function of the cells. I have found it very helpful for pain and many diseases. It would relax Buddy plus allow you to communicate with him during his last days." I explained several T-touch techniques and asked that she call me if she changed her mind about bringing Buddy in, or if I could help her further.

That afternoon, my receptionist rushed over to tell me that the lady was here with Buddy.

"I'm so glad you decided to bring Buddy in," I said. "Did you try the T-touch?"

"I sure did! And it worked in ways even you couldn't predict! While I was making little circles around his neck area, look what I found!" She held out a half-rotten, smelly rubber band.

"Oh, my! Let me guess. You have children, and one of them must

**101**

have put this rubber band around Buddy's neck!"

"That's right! And when I was doing the T-touch my fingers came back stinky and bloody when I got to the neck area, and that's how I discovered it. Thank goodness you told me how to do the T-touch massage!"

Well, I'm not sure we can connect this healing miracle to T-touch, but let's discuss what really happened to Buddy, and then I want to share with you the use of T-touch massage—it works with any animal, including humans.

⁂

It is common for children to put rubber bands around their animal's necks. They forget about them, and the rubber bands gradually dig into the flesh and cause ulcerations and infections. Usually the guardian can see that something is wrong, but Buddy was a long-haired dog, and there was nothing to see unless you parted his fur. He definitely would smell from rotten flesh; the woman had noted an odor, but thought dying dogs probably smelled. She hadn't thought to mention the smell to me. When the woman discovered it, she had removed the offending rubber band, so I had only to shave and treat the area. After two weeks of antibiotics, Buddy was just fine. Thank God he wasn't put to sleep!

⁂

T-touch is a type of massage that affects the nervous system. Linda

Tellington-Jones first perfected the technique on horses, then on people, then on dogs and cats. It has proven successful for behavior problems in animals such as barking, chewing, fear, aggressiveness, and nervousness, as well as for car sickness, shock, whelping difficulty, stiffness, recovery from injury, and almost all diseases.

Gentle vocal and physical contact alone for humans or animals is very beneficial. It dramatically decreases the heart rate and causes general relaxation of muscle tension. Soft "cooing" and massage also stimulate the parasympathetic nervous system; this stimulates the digestive system. This is why the tender loving care of a mother rocking her baby and singing it a lullaby, or a cat or dog licking its offspring or companion, facilitates the digestive process.

But T-touch accomplishes even more; it somehow awakens the body to heal itself. It's usually done with a circular touch (something about massaging in a circular pattern is critical for this to work). The person making the circles breathes into them as she makes them. These circles allow her to focus both her own and the animal's attention at the same time, allowing a deep sense of communion. Biofeedback shows that the person doing the massage registers brain waves known as "an awakened state" typical of healers and yogis. In England, where healers are invited to practice on patients in hospitals, it was noted that the brain waves of the person being massaged soon matched those of the healer.

People interested in reading more detail about brain waves should get Linda Tellington-Jones' book and tape. But suffice it to say that biofeedback machines and EEG machines show animals' brain waves also change when T-touch is being applied. While receiving T-touch massage, the animal's alpha, beta, theta, and delta waves show a definite connection between the subconscious and conscious thought—very odd, because usually people or animals have either conscious *or* subconscious brain waves, not both at the same time. This connection or bridge that is created between the conscious and subconscious is believed to open the "healer" within all of us and create the desired effect.

T-touch is not difficult to learn. First, try the following techniques out on your own body so you can judge how hard you need to press, then try them on a friend's arm and get her feedback. Then you are ready to try T-touch on your animal.

For arthritis and swelling, use a level 3 touch (1 is the lightest and 9 is the hardest one can push on the skin), doing what is called the "raccoon touch." Make small clockwise circles (making a complete circle plus another one-quarter turn, or 450 degrees) over the swollen or arthritic area. It's best to have shorter fingernails and cup your hand so that the ends of your fingers are actually doing the massage.

For aggression, aloofness, barking, car sickness, fear biting, leash pulling, nervousness, and reducing stress, do the "clouded leopard." This is done with a 4 pressure. Flatten your hand more than the method above, allowing a larger area of warm contact with extended fingers. The

*Raccoon touch*

*Clouded leopard*

weight of your hand rests lightly on the body, with fingers lightly curved. The pads of your fingers push the skin one and a quarter circle; the middle finger leads. Breathing quietly in rhythm with the circles helps maintain a softness in your fingers, hand, arm, and shoulder. Move the skin in a circle rather than rubbing over the hair. Make the circles all over the animal's body while he is sitting or lying down, especially over the hip region.

**105**

For arthritis, back problems, hip dysplasia, timidity, balance, and gait problems, aggression, biting, and fear of loud noises and thunder, do the "tail T-touch." Lift the animal's tail, following a straight line from the body and stroke down the tail several times to introduce the animal to handling the tail area. Using one hand near the base of the tail, slowly create an arch by pushing the tail upward, and move the tail around in a circle, rotating it in both directions. After several rotations in both directions, start at the rump and slide your hand down the tail in a series of pull-and-hold movements, each lasting four to six seconds. Continue to make small circles all the way down the tail.

At the end of any session, do the "Noah's march" to provide reintegration as well as revitalization of your companion animal. Beginning at

*Tail T-touch*

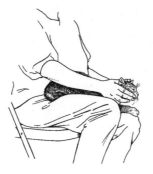

*Noah's march*

the head and neck, use long, sweeping strokes with the entire hand including the fingers and palms. Cover every inch of the body and tail and all the way down the legs to the end of the paws.

There are many studies proving that massage has positive effects on conditions from colic to hyperactivity to diabetes to migraines—in fact, every single physical malady has shown improvement with massage. It boosts immune function, helps asthmatics breathe easier, improves autistic children's ability to concentrate, and lowers anxiety.

But some people resist the idea that certain types of massage do in fact help to heal and ease pain. There's probably a deep reason for the resistance to accept the conclusions of all the research studies. America is what anthropologists call a "nontactile" society. Compared with most cultures we are "touchy" about touch. Observed rates of casual touch between people in Puerto Rico was 180 times per hour. In America the rate was two times per hour. Americans were more likely to fiddle with rings, crack their knuckles, twirl their hair, tap their faces, stroke their beards, or engage in other forms of self-stimulation. Americans aren't getting enough touch—and neither are American animals!

Cultures that show more physical affection toward infants and children tend to have lower rates of adult violence. And people who massage their babies tend not to abuse them. Touch is magical, whether for animals or people. So give Fido a massage and see what happens! 🕸

# The Skunk That
# Put on Airs

It was 8:00 in the evening of a busy day at work. Everyone was finishing up, their faces drawn and tired. The phone rang repeatedly. No one looked up—the answering service would get it. Ring! Ring! You can only ignore something like that for so long.

"It's the back line," said Patti with little enthusiasm. Ring! Ring!

"I'll get it," I said, trudging wearily toward it. "Hello?"

"Laura, thanks for answering."

"Oh, hi, Bob! What's up?" Bob was a good friend.

"You remember that skunk I was telling you about—the skinny one that was dragging his rear legs, looked like he'd been hit by a car or something?" he asked.

"Yeah," I said with resignation.

"Well, I trapped him in that humane trap you lent me. Can you come out and look at him—see if you can help him or at least put him out of his misery?" he asked.

"I don't suppose you'd be willing to bring him in?" I pleaded.

"No way I'm putting that smelly thing in my Beamer. You're the one that wanted me to catch him."

"Okay, I'll be right over. See ya," I said, setting down the receiver, my shoulders drooped and rounded from the news. The night had just grown longer.

"Need some help?" Patti said, grabbing her purse to leave.

"No, if it looks like we can help the skunk, I'll bring him back here and work on him. I should be able to manage by myself. Thanks. . . ." I realized she had already departed.

I got all my things ready—pen light, anesthetic agents, disinfectant and antibiotics, leather gloves, bandage material, and the like—and drove out to deal with the skunk.

As I drove up, Bob greeted me. "Did you bring a dart gun?"

"No, very few people have dart guns or permits to use them. I think the government is afraid we'll use them on IRS agents or something. But I brought some injectable anesthetics. You should be able to poke it in him through the cage," I said, nodding in affirmation.

"Me? I'll go with you, but I'm not giving no shot—no way!" he said, accentuating with his chin. "How are we going to get close enough to him to give the injection without being sprayed?" Good question—how were we?

We discussed and rejected various options, finally agreeing on a plan of action. Bob got large black garbage bags to protect our clothes; we made holes for our heads and arms and put them on. We donned towels on our heads to protect our hair should the skunk spray; Saran Wrap with holes for our eyes, noses, and mouths to protect our faces; and gloves for our hands. We each held a garbage can lid in front of us as shields, and in crouched positions courageously advanced on the caged skunk in the middle of the pasture.

About two yards from the skunk, I looked over at Bob crouched behind his garbage can lid, draped in his black bag, Saran-Wrapped face and toweled head, a flashlight clenched between his teeth, and I giggled. The sound must have startled our friend, because suddenly a yellowish-green obnoxious gas engulfed us. This odor was a hundred times stronger than what you smell as you drive by a road kill.

Blinded by our stinging tears, we hunched over, coughing and dry heaving. We thought we were going to die but were afraid we wouldn't—the smell was so vile. I heard a stream of expletives next to me, but couldn't make out Bob's form amid the caustic smoke.

Afraid Bob's profanity would trigger yet another aerosol bomb, I rushed forward with my syringe, poking through the cage at any part of the skunk I could reach. We ran back out of range, arguing all the while about what the "range" was, to a new source of oxygen while the anesthetic took effect.

The next few minutes were uneventful. The skunk passed out, and we examined her, deciding she had two broken hind legs—we should be able to help her. (Though I was more inclined to put her out of *our* misery, right at the moment.)

I decided I'd have to de-scent her at the time of the surgery to pin her legs. She'd need a lot of after-care, and there was no time to domesticate her so she wouldn't spray in fear. Using a large blanket, I wrapped up the cage and sleeping skunk and put her in my car.

(By the way, I never got that smell out of my car. Three years later, when I went to sell it, I remember the salesman saying with a look of repulsion on his face, "What is that smell?" when he examined the interior.)

I raced back to the hospital in my car; I definitely didn't want Señora Chlorophyll waking up. I hooked her up to an anesthetic machine and repaired her legs, then I proceeded to remove both scent glands.

The scent glands are located on each side of the anus—the same ones that are called anal glands in dogs. The glands have huge muscles so when contracted, the aerosolized substance can be ejected forcefully. When removing the glands, you have to be very careful not to nick the sacks, lest any of the vile-smelling dark yellow liquid leak out.

I knew just what this striped little lady could do, so I was proceeding with great caution, when I heard something at the window and looked up to see a man's face pressed up against it, looking straight at me. My hands jerked up. In that same microsecond, I realized it was Bob—he must have decided to come down and see how his rescuee was doing. But it was too late—I had dinged the gland.

For the second time that night, I was plunged into olfactory Hell.

The stench was so powerful I thought I might black out. The sharp needles of vapor caused my nose to produce copious mucus; my eyes swelled shut. I blindly groped my way out of the surgery suite.

After I stepped out into the night air to gulp frantically for air—and give Bob a piece of my mind—I went back into smell purgatory and finished the de-scenting.

My hospital was trashed. I hired fumigators, but I still had to close the hospital for three days, the stench was so bad. I bathed in gallons of tomato juice (supposed to get rid of skunk odors), but for weeks my presence caused pained expressions on those unfortunates around me. I had to cut my hair—couldn't get the stink out of it. The beautician insisted on cutting it in the parking lot—made some comment about needing fresh air. For over a month, clients would wrinkle their noses, and say, "Whew! Some poor dog got into a skunk, huh?"

I wasn't interested in reliving the story, so I would just shrug and say, "Yeah. The habits of skunks are phew! But unique."

❧ ❧ ❧ ❧

Remember the one about the skunk and her babies who got attacked by dogs? The mother skunk kneeled down and said to the babies, "Let us spray."

There are few smells as unpleasant—and penetrating—as skunk

spray. But there are some things you can do to decrease the chances of your dog getting sprayed.

Don't let your dog out at night—especially when there is a full moon. Skunks are nocturnal, and when there is a full moon, there is more light for the nocturnal animals to see for foraging food, so there will be more skunks out and for a longer period of time. (Porcupines—and their quills—also abound during full moons.)

Discourage skunks from making your house their home. Skunks like cool, dark areas, so clear away brush and piles of bricks or wood. Make sure there are no holes beneath your house for skunks to enter and set up housekeeping. If skunks are already in residence, wait until they wander out at night, then seal up the hole behind them. However, DON'T DO THIS IN THE SPRING—there are probably babies, and you don't want them to starve slowly without their mother. Skunks love dog and cat food, so don't leave your animals' food outside if you don't want to encourage skunks.

If your dog gets "skunked," here are some pointers. First, check his eyes; skunk spray is very irritating. It certainly won't blind him, as you sometimes hear, but it is painful. Rinse your dog's eyes with the same types of eyewash solutions people use.

Of course, bathe your dog (or your whole house will smell for weeks). Wear latex gloves to protect your hands from the smell and some sort of apron or protective clothing. The most common thing to use is tomato juice—use it straight out of the can (it'll take several large cans). Saturate the coat, and let it soak for approximately fifteen minutes before rinsing.

If your animal's fur is white, he will be an interesting shade of pink for a while after using this method. A good remedy for a white dog that has been sprayed is one-quarter cup of baking soda and one teaspoon of liquid soap in a quart of hydrogen peroxide. Work the solution into your animal's fur, then rinse well.

There are also many remedies at the pet store that work well, such as Skunk Kleen. But the product most animal groomers grab for skunked dogs is Massengill douche. For small to medium-sized animals, mix two ounces of Massengill with one gallon of water. For large dogs, double the amount of water and Massengill. Pour the mixture over the animal until it really soaks in, and wait fifteen minutes to rinse it out. Then wash him with regular shampoo and rinse thoroughly. ⚜

# Rico–The Pit Bull
of Birds

The parrot sat listless on the cage bottom, feathers all fluffed up. Things were looking bleak.

"He hasn't been eating, Doc. Rico's usually an ornery cuss—eager to bite me when I put food in his cage. But lately he just lays there and doesn't seem to notice me one way or another," said the rotund woman, her forehead glistening from the effort.

I started to get a pair of gloves, then decided against it after glancing at the motionless bird again. Rico looked barely alive—what danger could he pose? I reached into the cage, mentally cautioning myself to be very gentle. At that moment the bird came to life, as if just waiting for someone foolish enough to fall for his "playing dead" ploy.

His beak clamped onto one of my fingers with ferocity and determination, and a flame of excruciating pain blazed through my hand.

Not wanting to lose face with the client—after all, I was supposed to be a bird expert—I stifled my urge to scream and calmly removed my hand with the parrot at the end of it from the cage, as if that were how I always got birds out to examine them.

"I think Rico likes you. That's the most excited I've seen him in a couple of days," said the lady, her three chins wobbling in agreement.

I grabbed Rico with my free hand and tried prying his beak away from my finger. It worked, but with lightning speed he nailed the finger I was using as a crowbar—this parrot was the pit bull of the bird world.

I noticed the telltale red splotches on Rico's green feathers and realized I was bleeding profusely. Trying to maintain some semblance of dignity, I cocked my head to the side. "What?" I said as if hearing someone. "Okay, I'll be right there," I called out as if summoned outside the room. As I departed with Rico firmly affixed to my finger, I noticed the puzzled look on my client's face, but she said nothing.

After closing the exam room door behind me, I quickly ran to the nearest technician. "Quick, help me! Help me get this damn bird off my finger, will you?"

Together we managed to pry him off and put Band-Aids on my gaping wounds. With the bird firmly in hand, I returned to the exam room. My client quickly swallowed whatever snack she had just popped into her mouth. "Sorry for the interruption—they had a little problem they needed me for," I explained. I examined the bird and was startled to find a hard mass under the skin in the bird's groin area. Thinking it felt like an egg, I queried, "Are you sure Rico is a male? Could he possibly be a female?"

The client's eyes dilated as they radiated disapproval. "Of course, he's a male. I thought you were supposed to know about birds."

Humbled, I didn't respond for a few minutes, just continued examining the bird, giving myself time to think. "Well, it's most likely a tumor then. We should X-ray him and see how big it is and what organs might be involved."

The client frowned and chewed on her lip for a few seconds. I had the distinct impression she was trying to decide whether to leave her precious Rico with this stupid person who couldn't even tell a male from a female. Finally, she sighed, got up, and left me with Rico.

After setting up for the X ray, I tried to convince my technician to hold Rico while I took the X ray. Eyeing my mutilated hand, she quickly declined.

You can't wear gloves when X-raying a bird, because your hands cover too much of the bird and decrease what you can see on the X ray. So you usually tape the bird to the table, then take the X ray. Rico squawked, screeched, and struggled, but I finally managed to get him taped. "Okay, take it!" I yelled.

But before the tech could click the X ray, Rico ate the tape off his wings and was off the table, flying straight for me like a kamikaze pilot. I raised my hand to protect my face, and darned if he didn't latch onto another finger. I yelled, Rico shrieked, and we both hopped around the room, each damning the other in our own way.

Finally the tech came to my aid and we pried him off again, applying two new Band-Aids to my hands.

I then decided to put Rico inside a tube made of a gauze stockinet. I would hold the two ends, with him in the center, and take the X ray that way. I positioned him on the X-ray table. "Now!" I instructed. You could see him biting through the stockinet, and you could almost hear the *Jaws* theme song, "Dum Dum Dum Dum Dum Dum Dum Dum." "Hurry!" I shouted, not even trying to mask my panic.

I heard the hum of the machine and the click of the X ray being taken. A split second later, Rico was out of the stockinet—and you guessed it! His beak was now grinding on the web of my hand. I tried to dislodge him, but he just flapped his wings and dug his claws into my arm as he proceeded to saw with his beak.

As we performed our adversarial dance of war whoops, I told the technician to develop the X ray while I took Rico back to his person. I definitely didn't want to hold him any longer than absolutely necessary. Walking to the waiting room, I thought I had a firm hold of him, Lord knows I tried, but just as I was about to put Rico in his cage the woman was holding up imperiously, the bird got loose. And you guessed it, he attacked my fingers with a vengeance, clamping down with renewed vigor. In case you don't know, it *really* hurts to be bitten in the same place twice. Without thinking, I flicked my hand, trying to dislodge this avian monster.

"Don't hurt him! Don't hurt my Rico!" the woman demanded.

Just then I saw something fly through the air in a blur, hitting the woman with a splat! It was an egg! Rico WAS a female, and he, I mean, *she*, didn't have a tumor, just a retained egg—the yolk was on her!

 

&copy; &copy; &copy;

It is generally pretty easy for a veterinarian specializing in birds to sex them for you. Many birds are sexually dimorphic; that is, the male and female of the species are different in color. Most mistakes are made with immature birds that are declared females when in fact they are young males. For birds that aren't sexually dimorphic, there are two main ways to tell—surgery or blood feather analysis.

Sexing by surgical means involves the use of a laparoscope, an instrument (also used in human medicine) that has its own light source and is used to perform an internal examination of various parts of the body. The bird is anesthetized, then feathers are plucked from a small area behind the last rib on the left side. The area is cleaned with antiseptic, a small incision is made, and the laparoscope is inserted. A light source and transmitting cable illuminate the bird's internal organs to reveal ovaries or testes.

A young veterinarian, Dr. Marc Valentine, pioneered the method of sexing birds using a blood feather (one which is still growing and therefore has blood in the shaft) that is removed from the bird to be sexed. The pulp is removed from the feather shaft, and a cell culture is grown from the pulp. All that is required is one blood quill (perhaps two for a small bird), which must be kept sterile and must reach the laboratory within twenty-four hours. After seven to ten days, enough cells have grown in the culture to enable a chromosome preparation to be made. The chromosomes are then analyzed, thus determining the sex, and also demonstrating whether the bird possesses any chromosomal defects. For example, some birds are genetically intersex (neither male nor female) and are therefore sterile. Outwardly normal, this could never be discovered in any other manner. Many people try to guess their bird's sex by its behavior, but this is very deceiving. This is one time when communing with animals will not necessarily give you your desired results. You just can't tell a bird's sex by its behavior.

❧ ❧ ❧ ❧ ❧

Do you want a tip on how to be a Bird Whisperer? Have you ever tried to tame a bird that won't let you near him without attacking? Put on gloves, and the bird gets even more frantic and aggressive. Reach in with your bare hands, and suffer the consequences. Here is a training trick used by falconers for centuries: Stroke the bird with feathers.

Falconers sit up all night, continuously stroking a wild bird with a feather to keep him awake but calm. By morning, the bird, defenses worn down, will be tame.

Hands are threatening to a wild bird, but a long feather establishes contact without scaring him. It is best to use two slightly stiff feathers (you can buy them at a hobby shop or obtain them from someone who has chickens), one on each side of the bird, to desensitize him. Stroke the bird on both sides until he no longer resists the contact; gradually move your fingers up the feather, so they are closer and closer to the bird. Then lightly stroke the bird with a finger on one side and a feather on the other. Birds have a natural fear of predators coming from above, so always approach the bird with your hands and fingers at eye level or lower to minimize his "fleeing" response. In an amazingly short time, you will be able to handle the bird after feather stroking; this is actually a variation of Linda Tellington-Jones' T-touch technique for calming animals. ❁

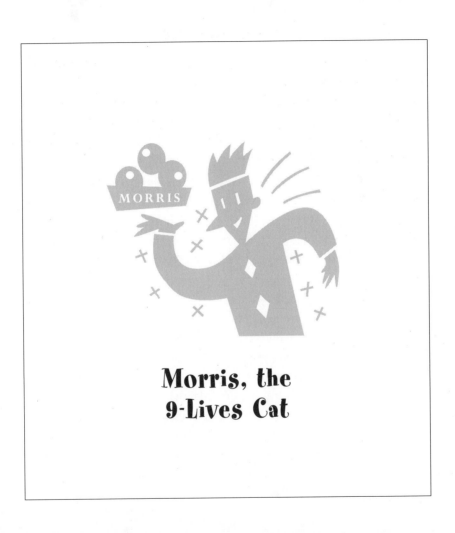

# Morris, the
# 9-Lives Cat

 I was lucky enough to be the veterinarian for Morris, the 9-Lives Cat, for a number of years. I even got a pilot's license and bought an airplane (which has a drawing of Morris and the words *Morris Airlines* painted on the plane's tail) to transport Morris to various publicity functions. I thought you might enjoy reading the answers to the most frequently asked questions about him. And I thought I'd also share a little-known secret about this finicky feline.

The present Morris is Morris #2. (There is a Morris #3 being groomed as a fill-in.) Morris #1 lived to be nineteen years old, and Morris #2 is going on twenty years old. Both Morrises were rescued from New England animal shelters just prior to being put to sleep. Morris #2 weighs approximately twenty-four pounds and lives near Chicago with his handler/trainer, Bob Martwick.

When Star-Kist, which owns 9-Lives, was selecting the original Morris, they had five to six finalists—felines of various colors and types. One at a time, these cats were placed on a big conference table surrounded by executives; whoever was the group's favorite would spearhead their advertising campaign. Each cat presented was discussed and evaluated for its appeal, et cetera. When it was Morris' turn, he didn't just stand there or leap off the table like the others. No, he slowly strutted up and down the table sizing *them* up. With tremendous insight—or luck—he stopped in front of the CEO, and butted the head of this top executive. (Morris always greeted his favorite people by head-butting them.) He then proceeded to sit in front of the startled man in his most regal and haughty stance. He was, of course, picked on the spot and soon became a television superstar worth millions.

There was a different selection process for Morris #2. One of the main criteria was for the cat to be able to tolerate loud noises, bright studio lights, and crowds. A test was devised where the five finalists—all large orange felines—were lined up on a cement floor. Someone threw a metal feed dish on the floor behind them, which made a loud clatter. All of the cats yowled and sprang away—all but one, that is. Morris #2 just looked back toward the pan with disdain and contempt. That was it—he had that elusive "star quality."

Here's Morris #2's secret: he *loves* martini olives! It's true, I saw it for myself! One night at a food broker party, Morris was sitting proudly in his Morris Production Chair as people posed next to him getting their picture taken. A lady with a martini in her hand leaned in for a snapshot, and Morris stole that olive quicker than any pickpocket. There were a number of people with martinis, and any time one of them came within a yard of him, he stealthily swiped the olives. I asked his trainer, Bob

Martwick, about it; he said, "Morris is crazy about martini olives—not just green olives, but olives soaked in martinis."

I've asked feline behaviorists, and it seems a martini olive has an effect much like catnip to a cat. I've looked into it, Morris, and there is presently an AA for little alcoholics—it's called "aa."

☙ ☙ ☙ ☙

You know your cat has a drinking problem when he won't drink out of his water bowl unless there's an olive in it! Many cats like olives; it could be the preservatives, or cats may like them because they can bat them around. Most cats don't like martinis, but many like beer. What would turn an ordinary house cat into a party animal? Cooper and Noble, in *277 Secrets Your Cat Wants You to Know,* say that part of it is that the yeasty taste of olives attracts cats. They relate a story about Trixi, a cat that lived with pub owners in Wales. They couldn't figure out what was wrong with Trixi—her vet treated her for various things. Then they discovered she had really developed a taste for beer and that she spent most of her time beneath the pub's drip trays behind the bar. They found her staggering about drunk one day and realized her problem was alcohol poisoning.

Sometimes you can't tell if your animal is drunk; it never occurs to you since you're not the one to give him alcohol (it's usually a prank by a teenager). The symptoms are bleary eyes, listlessness, staggering, or acting like a person with a bad headache. Sound familiar?

◈◈◈◈◈

Have you ever heard the expression, "Cure a hangover with the hair of the dog"? It means that some people believe that having a small drink on the morning after a drunken night might help to cure a hangover. The phrase "hair of the dog" comes from eighteenth-century folklore that professed that the very thing that caused the pain would also cure it; so, it was believed that "the hair of the dog" that gave the wound should be applied to the part injured.

◈◈◈◈◈

Speaking of dog hair, here's a little trick. Dog hair (from combing or clipping) and/or a scoop of dog feces placed down a mole hole will usually make the pests change residences. Don't tell your neighbor you did this, however; he will hate you when the moles move next door.

Here's another tip about dog hair. Do you have one of those dogs that wake you up at some ungodly hour? (I consider anything earlier than 7:00 A.M. to be ungodly.) The next time your dog wakes you up too early, clean out some of the hair in his outer ear canal, using a pair of tweezers. It's good to clean out these hairs anyway, since they encourage the entrance of foxtails into the ear; they also decrease the air that gets into the ear and therefore encourage infections. But that isn't the real reason you have decided to clean his ears when he wakes you up too early. Dogs hate to have their ears fussed with. If every time your dog wakes you up early he realizes you are going to be fussing with his ears (trimming toenails works well also), he will soon wait for you to get up on your own.

◈ ◈ ◈ ◈ ◈

No discussion of feline cravings can leave out catnip. Behaviorist Desmond Morris says that roughly 50 percent of cats love catnip, and the other 50 percent are indifferent to it. Whether they are ecstatic about it is genetic—training or conditioning has nothing to do with it. He says that kittens under three months of age are indifferent to catnip, but after three months of age, 50 percent go wild over it. These cats sniff it, then with growing frenzy start to lick, bite, chew, and rub against it repeatedly. The cats purr loudly, growl, roll over, and even leap in the air. The catnip plant, a member of the mint family, contains an oil called hepetalactone, an unsaturated lactone that does for some cats what marijuana does for some people.

Catnip (*Nepeta catania*) is not the only plant to produce these strange reactions in cats. Valerian (the herb they use to make Valium) is another one, and there are several more that have strong cat appeal. It is interesting to note that catnip or valerian administered internally acts as a tranquilizer, but when inhaled is a stimulant.

And finally, talking about Morris, the 9-Lives Cat, do you know why people say a cat has nine lives? Of course, a cat's resilience, independence, ability to land on its feet, and ability to take care of itself lead people to believe it is blessed with many lives. But do you know why we say *nine* lives? In ancient times nine was considered a particularly lucky number, because it was a "trinity of trinities" and therefore ideally suited for the lucky cat. ☀

**Angry Bulls Charge
Vegetarians Also**

On my way to work one day, I saw a large dead raccoon in the middle of the road. I pulled over to the side and approached the poor thing to move him to the grass nearby—I hate to see the body of a dead animal further mutilated by traffic. I was amazed to learn he was still breathing, though unconscious and in obvious shock. I thought that with some emergency therapy he had a chance, so I carefully scooped him up and took him to my car. I put him in my lap, so he'd get some of my body heat (heat is important to combat shock) and drove toward my veterinary hospital.

My office was only about ten minutes away, but five minutes into the drive, my patient woke up! And I don't mean that he started blinking or groggily moving about—he was wide awake! It wasn't like a Disney movie where the animal blinks and looks into your eyes with adoration for trying to save him—this 'coon was looking at me with hatred and revenge—preparing to attack as if he were sure I were responsible for his condition. All forty pounds of him were snarling and snapping inches from my face, his long canines glistening with possibly rabies-tainted saliva, his hair bristled, and his ears pulled back tight against his head.

I squealed to a stop and gave the passenger door a shove—praying he'd just leap out rather than lunge toward my face. Agonizing moments passed when he seemed undecided whether to attack or flee. I just froze, averting my eyes so as not to look challenging, and started saying my mental "Hail Mary"s. He finally ambled out toward the forest.

A car in the opposite lane had stopped to watch me open the door and let an adult raccoon out as if for his daily stroll. The driver looked at me quizzically, seeking an explanation. I just gave a lopsided grin and shrugged my shoulders, shut the door, and drove off. I've often wondered what the other driver thought.

❧ ❧ ❧ ❧

Thinking about how that raccoon snarled and hissed reminded me that the similarity between the hiss of a cat and that of a snake is not accidental—it is a case of protective mimicry. In other words, the cat imitates the snake to give an enemy the impression that it too is venomous and dangerous.

The sound of a cat hissing when threatened by a dog or some other predator does sound almost identical to that of a threatened snake. Predators have an inborn respect for venomous snakes—they don't have to learn to avoid them. (Learning would not be of much use, as the first lesson would also be the last.) If a cornered cat (or other animal, such as

**135**

a raccoon) is capable of causing alarm in an attacker by triggering this instinctive fear of snakes, it obviously has a great advantage, and this is probably the true explanation of why the feline hiss has evolved.

Supporting this idea is the fact that cats often add spitting to hissing—spitting is another way in which threatened snakes react. Also, the cornered cat may twitch or thrash its tail in a special way, reminiscent of the movements of a snake that is working itself up to strike or flee.

There is another similarity between snakes and cats. When a tabby cat (with markings like the ancestral cat) lies sleeping, curled up tightly on a tree stump or rock, its coloration and its rounded shape make it look uncannily like a coiled snake. As long ago as the nineteenth century, it was suggested that the pattern of markings on a tabby cat are imitations of the camouflage markings of a snake. A killer, such as an eagle, seeing a sleeping cat might, as a result of this resemblance, think twice before attacking. ✿

**Clean Out Your Cupboards so the Ants Have to Eat Out**

**T**he man entered the exam room with his Maine Coon cat tucked under his arm. "He just needs his shots," he said.

I did a physical on the cat, and all seemed well, except the animal seemed a little thin and dehydrated. I mentioned this to his guardian; he reminded me that the cat was fourteen years old, and vowed to encourage him to eat more.

I vaccinated the cat as requested and was about to dismiss the client, when he said, "Oh, and by the way, I need some flea spray or something to kill all the damned ants around the house."

After questioning the man, I found out that the ants were especially plentiful around the cat's litter box. It suddenly occurred to me why the cat was thin and dehydrated. I convinced the man to let me do a blood test, and sure enough—the cat was diabetic! The ants had been attracted to the sugar in the urine of the diabetic cat! Sometimes in life, when you have a problem, it's as important to find out *why* you have the problem as it is to solve it.

And to find out why there is a problem as well as how to cure it (rather than just treat or get rid of the symptoms), you should use

Western medicine as well as holistic and alternative approaches. I believe that in the near future most doctors *will* combine Western, Eastern, and holistic medicine—they'll be prescribing fluoridated chicken soup or something.

❧ ❧ ❧ ❧ ❧

An example of an Eastern medicine technique is one taught by Anitra Frazier called the "almost" touch. It is stroking just above your animal's body—to within a half-inch of touching him (some people refer to this as "aura stroking"). You will often be able to tell that there is an altered energy sensation where there is a physical problem. Hold both hands palm down over the area that feels different, again still not touching the animal's body. The sensations in your palms increase and may feel hot, cold, vibrating, or you may feel an electrical feeling or other sensations. Shake the energy or feelings out of your hands, then put them above the trouble spot again. You will notice that the odd energy or sensation has been lessened or removed. Repeat the process until stroking just above every part of your animal (including his legs) produces homogenous or the same electrical feelings in the palm of your hands.

I think it's also helpful to utilize chakras or major energy networks in your animal's body. Hands (or your head) placed on chakras will also deepen telepathic communication between human and animal. If the animal is cooperative, place your head on your animal's forehead (crown/brow chakra) or place your hands on the animal's chest (solar plexus) or belly.

◎ ◎◎ ◎◎ ◎◎

Many people have had success using color with their healing techniques—that is, they imagine sending rays of colored light from their hands to the animal's body. Diane Stein tells us that blue or green, the universal healing colors, soothe an animal that is in pain. A depleted animal welcomes life-force red to warm and vitalize. An animal in need of love and calming trust responds to pink, rose, red-violet, or violet. Metallic gold is good for infectious diseases and intensive healing, and metallic silver for healing broken or injured bones. A good rule in using color is to visualize and send it only as "light" allowing it to become whatever color is best for the animal's needs.

To do distant healing or communication, get into a meditative state. Imagine the dog or cat standing in front of you; Diane Stein states that it will not be a photographic image, but either a silhouette or a fuzzy representation. When you have the image, ask in your mind what the animal needs, even if you already know. Then ask for permission to do healing to help him. If he agrees to accept energy from you, either send light and color as described earlier or imagine that you are physically there with your animal, doing the healing with your hands. Diane tells us to visualize that the dog or cat is resting in your lap, or that the cat's or dog's head

**140**

is on your knee; then do the "laying on of hands" healing on your knee, focusing the energy to reach your animal. If the dog has a cut or injury, sew it up with a Goddess needle and thread. If there is fever, visualize a thermometer with the high reading; pile imaginary ice around the thermometer and the animal, and watch the reading drop to normal. Before leaving the meditation, visualize the cat or dog as completely well and healed.

I have to share with you one experience I had communicating with a puppy who was about to be euthanized at an animal shelter. I often go to our local Humane Society on the day that animals are being put to sleep, trying to love and cuddle each one so that at least their last moments are loving ones. Like many other people, I rescue as many as I can, but it's getting so that when someone sees me, they raise their hands and say, "No, I can't take another dog or cat!"

This particular day, a small black Labrador-mix puppy looked particularly dejected and forlorn as he waited with the other dogs in the bin to be rolled into the vacuum chamber to be put to sleep. I picked him up and stroked him gently and told him what a good puppy he was, and that I was so sorry that someone hadn't been lucky enough to adopt him. His big brown eyes searched mine, as if he was trying to communicate. I closed my eyes and tried to empty my thoughts to receive his. It hit me with a jolt—the most vivid colored picture I have ever had with an animal—he was thinking of the only happy memory in his short life: his mother tenderly licking and loving him.

Of course, I had to rescue just one more. That little guy got a great home; his guardian named him Splash (he loves water) and values him like no other—swears Splash is the smartest and best dog he's ever had. And, yes, Splash and his guardian regularly communicate using the techniques described above. ☀

# The Dog Who Wore
# the Pants in the Family

A man called a veterinarian at midnight to say a neighbor's mongrel had mounted his purebred dog. The vet said, "Throw a bucket of water on them and squirt them with a hose." The man said he tried, and it didn't work. The vet then said, "Well, put the phone down near the dogs, and I'll call you." "Will that work?" the man asked. The veterinarian replied, "Well, it worked here!"

This silly joke reminded me of Cricket, the Cocker Spaniel. Cricket was one year old when she had her first heat cycle. Her mistress was totally distraught—she scheduled an appointment so we could discuss this delicate subject in the privacy of my office.

I explained that dogs have a three-week cycle during which females can possibly conceive. "Why don't we spay her now?" I asked.

She looked at me with utter disbelief. "Spay her? I spent $600 for her. She has exquisite bloodlines. Why would I spay her?" I caught her sneaking a look at my diploma on the wall.

"Cricket is really a beautiful Cocker," I hastened to reassure her. "But she's too young to breed for at least another year—that's two heat cycles where you have to be certain she doesn't get bred accidentally. And raising the puppies and finding good homes is a bit of work. I just didn't know you were planning to breed her."

Her face had the look of someone who just smelled something vile. "I just told you I paid $600 for her—of course I'm going to breed her! Now, what can I do to make sure some horrid dog doesn't force her to . . . you know."

"Well, we can give her chlorophyll tablets. . . ."

"Chlorophyll? Her breath is just fine! Maybe I should talk to another veterinarian. . . ."

I told her how taking chlorophyll would decrease the distance from which male dogs could smell Cricket's fertile state. I explained how Cricket would always have to be on a leash when she went potty— because she might run off to be with a male.

The woman, of course, said Cricket would never do that—but wanted to know how they could prevent some male dog from jumping on top of poor Cricket before they could chase him off.

I told her that many people put a pair of women's underwear on their dog, with a hole cut out for the tail. I reminded her that she'd need to remove the underwear to allow the dog to eliminate.

She stood up, signaling our conversation was over, glaring at my diploma on the wall again.

Two weeks later she returned, red-faced and hyperventilating, holding Cricket. "It didn't work! That nasty awful beagle-something down the street jumped her before I could stop him. Now what do I do?" She walked over to my diploma and openly scrutinized it.

I had to bite my lip to keep from laughing. There, under her arm, was Cricket, wearing a pair of red thong bikinis—probably from Frederick's. The Cocker Spaniel was definitely more exposed than covered. It taught me never to assume that all women wear underwear like my grandmother's.

◎ ◎◎ ◎◎ ◎◎

Getting stuck is a natural part of dog's mating and is called "tying." At the base of a dog's penis is a gland called the *bulbus glandis,* and once it has entered the female, it starts to swell. At the same time the female's vagina becomes strongly constricted. This forms the powerful lock or "tie." When the male is done, he is still "tied" to the female for approximately twenty minutes. During this awkward time, he usually lifts one of his hind legs over the female's neck and turns away from her, so the pair stands tied together, but facing in opposite directions. This allows them to have defenses or "teeth" at both ends while they are in this vulnerable position.

The purpose of the tie is that dogs ejaculate differently than humans. Instead of a simple, single, relatively brief ejaculate as with humans, a dog ejaculates in three phases, which takes approximately twenty minutes.

The first phase takes approximately forty-five seconds; this ejaculate is a clear, spermless fluid. The second phase takes about ninety seconds; this ejaculate is thick and white and contains approximately 1,250 million sperm. The third phase continues as long as the tie persists (approximately twenty minutes); it involves a much larger quantity of ejaculate that is clear and spermless. This is the prostatic fluid that pushes the sperm into the female's reproductive tract as well as activates the sperm that have just been deposited there.

≈ ೨೦ ೨೦ ೨೦

By the way, did you hear that veterinarians now prescribe birth control pills for dogs? It's part of an anti-litter campaign (just kidding). I would like to add my voice to that of Roger Caras, president of the SPCA, who is trying to get people to call mixed breeds "random-bred dogs" rather than mongrels. That way, there would be purebred and random-bred dogs; it gives them a little more dignity.

≈ ೨೦ ೨೦ ೨೦

People often ask me about how to stop their little dogs from mounting their legs or cushions. Masturbating is a perfectly normal canine activity, and since he considers you as part of the pack, your dog will often include you in this action. Some dogs have their favorite cushion

**147**

and will carry it to a quiet corner for a little stimulation, while others, depending upon their size, prefer human elbows, knees, or legs—some male dogs even have favorite stuffed toys for this purpose.

Most people find it offensive and disturbing, so you should train your dog that this is not appropriate behavior. A stern "NO!" from a person, combined with a minute's isolation in a quiet and empty room each time a dog masturbates, will usually eliminate the behavior within a few weeks. If a young dog is not reprimanded when he first starts masturbating, it soon becomes a firmly ingrained habit and is more difficult to overcome. ✳

# I See Why She Can't See

The little gray-haired lady was frail and vulnerable as she sat hunched over, desperately clutching and protecting her precious burden. Every once in a while you could see her back quiver and shake, and then she absentmindedly wiped her cheeks with an unsteady blue-veined hand. I called her name; she furtively glanced around and laboriously started the process of getting up. She stood there swaying and tottering for a second, gathering all her strength and dignity—trying to tell herself that it was going to be okay. But it was *not* going to be okay. Emma Harris was about to put to sleep the only living thing she loved, the only living thing that loved her—Monet, her Persian cat.

Mrs. Harris shuffled into the exam room, and I thought my heart would break. My receptionist had already warned me that she was going to put her cat to sleep because Monet had gone blind.

I remembered comforting Mrs. Harris a year ago when her husband died after a prolonged battle with cancer. And it was only two months ago that Emma had found her fifteen-year-old Chihuahua, Jock, dead in his little bed. My eyes misted as I remembered how Mrs. Harris had tenderly carried Jock in so that she could be certain that nothing could be done for him.

But nothing could be done for Jock; he had died in his sleep, leaving Monet to watch over their beloved mistress.

And now, here she was again—she couldn't bear to see Monet blind and miserable. Many animals get along just fine blind, but not Monet—she bumped into things; sat in the middle of the floor, and meowed plaintively for her mistress to come pick her up. She either couldn't find her food or had lost interest in it, because Mrs. Harris could feel Monet's little body becoming pitifully thin. Monet, who had once been fastidiously clean, now rarely groomed herself and often didn't bother to track down the litter box.

"No," Emma Harris said aloud. "I love her too much to put Monet through anymore. I must put my little girl (she often referred to Monet as 'Mamma's little girl') to sleep."

She reached into her pocket and brought out an already used McDonald's napkin and blew her nose softly as she absentmindedly petted Monet with her other hand.

I chuckled at the napkin. Emma Harris was a thrifty lady. In fact, I thought, Emma might be a *very* thrifty lady! I could barely get the words out fast enough. "Aah, Mrs. Harris, what did you do with Jock's leftover food after he died? Did you by any chance feed it to Monet?"

She looked puzzled, but answered, "Yes, why?"

The world suddenly looked brighter. Mrs. Harris had been feeding her cat Jock's dog food! Monet had probably developed a deficiency of an amino acid called taurine and had developed central retinal degeneration or blindness as a result. And since Monet had been on this diet less than three months, it was quite possible that the condition was reversible!

"Mrs. Harris," I practically shouted, "we might be able to cure Monet's blindness—in fact there is a good chance we can!"

She searched my eyes for a ray of hope. "Really, Doctor? Really? How could that be?"

I explained that cats' nutritional needs are very unique and different from dogs. Cats, unlike dogs, need taurine in their diet. And when they don't get it, they can develop blindness or heart disease. Taurine is added to commercial cat food, but not to dog food. "It's quite possible, Mrs. Harris, that if we start Monet on a high quality commercial cat food right now we can reverse the blindness."

"You mean that Monet might see again? That I wouldn't have to put my little girl to sleep?"

"That's exactly what I mean," I said with a smile.

Emma Harris did her best version of a skip with her little arthritic legs and promised to get Monet some cat food immediately.

One month went by before I saw Mrs. Harris again—or was it her younger sister? There was a big smile on her face, and she was smartly dressed—life was worth living after all!

She gave me a big hug of gratitude, and, of course, some preserves she had canned herself, and told me how well her little girl was doing. She said Monet was her old self again—she could see! She told me how Monet proudly spent hours grooming her beautiful fur, and how, when it was time to eat, Monet lead the way jauntily with her tail straight in the air, as if to say, "This is the way, Mom."

My eyes lifted upward, and I murmured, "Thank you."

"What?" said Mrs. Harris.

I smiled warmly and said, "I'm so glad. I'm so very, very glad. Now, don't forget to bring Monet in for her vaccines."

"Oh, I won't," Mrs. Harris assured. "Well, Monet and I have to be off. Our favorite program, *The Young and the Restless,* comes on in a few minutes, and we never miss it. Good-bye, and God bless you," she said earnestly as she hurried out the door.

My heart swelled at the thought of all the happy moments Emma and Monet would be able to share together. "God bless you," I whispered.

☙ ❧ ❧ ❧

Yes, Monet had truly been blind as a bat. Have you ever wondered why people say "blind as a bat"? Bats aren't blind, but are quite capable of using their eyes if the sun isn't bright. It's a bonus that they can also navigate by sonar, emitting squeals and listening for echoes. The original saying was "blind as a bat at noon" which made sense, because bright light bothers bats (even though it doesn't blind them).

Bats are really cute little furry mice with wings, but their nocturnal habits and eerie cries frighten many people. By and large they pose no threat to human beings. They eat mostly fruit and insects. There are, however, blood-sucking "vampire" bats in Central and South America. (It is interesting that in Eastern Europe, home of the vampire legends, there are no vampire bats.) Vampire bats seem to prefer the blood of chickens, cows, and horses to human blood. But if a vampire bat takes a liking to your hemoglobin, he will repeatedly seek you out. Fortunately, you wouldn't feel a thing, because his saliva acts as a local anesthetic.

⚬ ⚬ ⚬ ⚬ ⚬

In our discussion of blindness and eyes, this is probably a good place to discuss the third eyelids or *haws* of cats. Many clients call in a panic because they think their cat's eye is ruptured and sunken, when, in fact, all that is wrong is that the third eyelid is raised, so the person can see only one-half of the eye. The haw or third eyelid (also called nictitating membrane) is located in the inner corner of the eye (in human eyes, there is just a remnant of this—it looks like a small pink lump at the inner part of the eye). In dogs and cats, this eyelid can go up to cover the entire eye to protect it or to lubricate the corneal surface by spreading ocular fluid evenly across the eye. Cats, especially when suffering from a

**154**

foreign body such as a foxtail in the eye, when tranquilized, or when in ill health, undernourished, or about to succumb to a major disease, display a constant raised third eyelid, giving the eye a "half-shuttered" look. When there is an injury to the cornea, such as a scratch or foxtail, the third eyelid is raised to protect the eye. When tranquilized, the third eyelid is raised because of ocular muscle relaxation. But when the cat is ill or undernourished, the third eyelid is raised because the shock absorber pads of fat behind the eye start to shrink. The eye then sinks deeper into the socket, which moves the third eyelid forward, covering half of the eye. When the cat returns to full health again, the fat pads are replenished and the eyes are pushed forward, hiding the third eyelid again.

◈◈◈◈◈

To give dogs equal time, there is one aspect about their eyesight that is important for communication. Unlike humans' eyes, dogs' eyes are more sensitive to movement and less so to detail. If something stands still a good distance from them, it becomes almost invisible. This is why so many of their prey, like rabbits, "freeze" and stand motionless when they become alarmed. It has been proven that if a dog's guardian stands motionless 300 yards from his dog, the dog can't detect him. Yet, as far away as one mile from the dog, a person can be detected if he is making bold hand signals (again, because dogs' eyes are more sensitive to movement than detail). So, in regards to communication, if you are at the beach trying to get your dog to return, don't just stand there yelling at him—make broad, quick gestures to get his attention while calling him. ☀

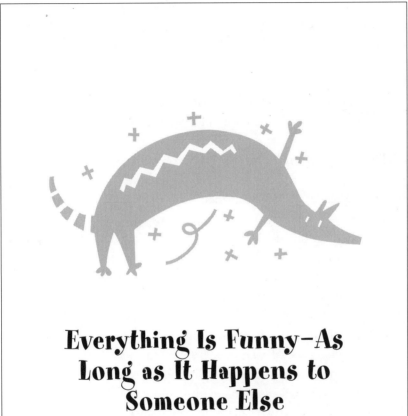

# Everything Is Funny–As Long as It Happens to Someone Else

In addition to my veterinary hospital, I have a certified wildlife rehabilitation facility; therefore, I am always raising and releasing orphaned wildlife. Loggers often bring in litters of raccoons they find in trees they've downed. I raise the baby raccoons on bottles, and when they are ready to wean, I start leaving their cage door open so they can run around outside and practice climbing trees and being self-sufficient. Usually, they stay out all night, coming back during the daytime for their bottle; as they get older, they miss more and more feedings until eventually they don't return.

This story is about a pair of orphaned baby raccoons I raised named Daniel Coon and Robbie. All raccoons are curious, intelligent, and whimsical, but these two were especially mischievous. They were always into everything—they'd take their baby bottles apart and chortle with glee to see the milk spill out; their little dexterous hands would sneak through the wire cage and fiddle with the locks, seeking a way to freedom. When outside, they'd hang from railings by one hand like monkeys, then one would jump piggyback on the other; in mock battle they'd fall in a furry ball, chortling in delight. They'd turn on faucets, making little washing motions with their hands in the water, then they'd pounce and splash in the water, like children playing in a mud puddle. Their favorite activity was to ride on your shoulders, their hands around your forehead for support, and if you jumped around, they'd chortle in ecstasy.

One day my next-door neighbor, Dick, met me at the fence, a look on his face I couldn't quite interpret. He had this story to tell.

◈ ◈◈ ◈◈ ◈◈

It was a dark, moonless night. Dick walked outside to put some trash in his garbage can. Suddenly, he felt something big and hairy jump on his head and start digging its sharp nails into his neck and face. He screamed and lunged, swatting at the animal in his attempts to dislodge it. He was certain it was some rabid creature that was going to bite and slash his face, permanently scarring him while transmitting the fatal disease. The more he beat at the animal, the tighter the animal's nails dug into his shoulders. He started to run toward the house, but before he'd taken more than a step or two, another animal clawed its way up his leg, digging into his chest on its way to join the other creature on his head. By now, Dick's heart was pounding thunderously, barely contained within his chest. His shrieks brought his wife running; one of the creatures jumped on her back, and Dick and his wife proceeded to jump, twist, swat, run, and shriek in the moonless night. Somehow they managed to get to their back door, dislodge their attackers, and slam the screen door shut as the furry devils lunged at them. The animals proceeded to hang from the screen by their claws screaming in fury that their prey had gotten away.

Dick and his wife called 911.

"Help! We've just been attacked by rabid animals! Need help—shoot them! Ambulance! Come now! 265 Talking Pines Road."

Assured help was on its way, they no sooner hung up when they heard a loud banging noise on the side of the house. Thump! Thump! Thump! They turned on the outside lights and saw a raccoon sitting in one of the planters hanging from the eaves. He was pushing off from the house, then riding the planter into the side of the house—thump—only to push off again. Another raccoon climbed up to the planter and proceeded to uproot the flowers, attempting to stick them in his ears. Dick and his wife realized the raccoons were just mischievous babies, not rabid killers, so they called 911 again and canceled the call.

I apologized for the raccoons and told Dick, "Thank goodness you love animals and have a sense of humor. Otherwise, Fish and Game would have been on my doorstep demanding I become a nun."

"A nun?" he said.

"Yes, you know . . . 'nun' of this and 'nun' of that."

⊚ ᏽ ᏽ ᏽ

This obviously wasn't a real animal attack; Robbie and Daniel Coon were just playing. But what if a dog or cat attacks you? I have a couple of tips.

Have you ever noticed that some people are able to soothe a barking or suspicious dog, and other people can't? Usually, the difference is how the people move. Some people have naturally smooth movements—others, by nature, are rather tense and jerky. Quick, hesitant movements arouse suspicion and aggression in animals. People who get along with dogs answer the dog's greeting with fluid approaches rather than jerky withdrawals. They walk confidently toward the dog and offer gentle hand contact. So, if a dog seems nervous or about to attack, slow your movements down, act confident, and continue walking purposefully. A confident posture emboldens you and disarms the dog (and gives courage to the soul). Do not ignore the dog. Many people mistakenly try to ignore the dog, which will often cause an attack, because the dog is trying to get your attention and respect. Put a smile on your face (even if you don't feel it), and in a conversational, soothing tone tell the dog, "*Goooood* fella. What a *goooood* watchdog you are. It's *aaall* right." Talking in a comforting, rhythmical tone has an effect similar to petting or massaging the dog. In addition, it will automatically slow down your breathing and movement, thereby calming and steadying you. If he should growl menacingly, continue your slow, purposeful walking. Look at him briefly and in a deep, authoritative voice (don't shout) say, "Stop that. What a silly boy you are." When he stops growling for a second, say, "That's better. Good boy!" Most dogs will be confused by this and will let you continue on your way, because you are treating them with respect and don't appear to be a threat or enemy.

☙ ☙ ☙

Have you ever noticed that your cat sometimes won't have anything to do with you, or dislikes a friend of yours? It could be because of a product you or your friend are wearing that day. Many products we use are developed from animals, and cats are very sensitive to these odors and can react badly to them. (Perhaps the animal scent in the product is a challenge to the cat?) To get you thinking about what the offending odor could be, I'll mention just two products—lanolin, which is found in many cosmetic items (remember, it comes from sheep), and lipstick, which may contain fish scales. Try to avoid wearing animal products around such sensitive felines.

Have you ever wondered why cats seem to be attracted to people who dislike them? If a cat enters a room filled with several people, he is very likely to head for the one person who hates or fears cats. To that person's horror, the cat proceeds to rub around his legs and may even jump up on the person's lap. Some people believe it's because the cat is inherently wicked, but the explanation is simpler than that.

When the cat enters the room and looks around, he notices several people staring at him—cat lovers who are gazing at him because they want his attention. But, in feline terms, to be stared at is to be mildly threatened—staring is rude. The only person not threatening him with a stare is the person who sees the cat, then looks away and stays very still, trying to be ignored by the feared animal. For the cat, in search of a friendly lap on which to sit, it heads for this ideal companion—someone not staring, not moving around or talking loudly. So the secret for any cat-phobic person who wants cats to stay away is to lean toward a cat and stare fixedly at him, while making agitated hand movements.

◈ ◈◈ ◈◈ ◈◈

Have you ever noticed how your cat greets you? The cat presses against you with his head, then rubs his flank and maybe tail around you, looks up and repeats the process, then wanders off, sits down, and washes his flank fur. The cat has special scent glands on the temples and at the gape of the mouth, and at the root of the tail. Your cat has marked you with its scent from these glands. The cat then interprets our scent signals he got while rubbing by sitting down and "tasting" us with his tongue. ❁

**163**

# A Woman Who Does
# Surgery on an Elephant
# Is a Big Operator

With the circus music blaring and people laughing at the clowns' antics, the grand finale arrived. All of the elephants had to sit up on cue. As Bubbles sat on his haunches, there were startled looks on the faces of the people in the front row. Some were looking down at their clothes, some were staring intently at Bubble's trunk, and others seemed to be searching the ring for a source of water. You see, the front row was drenched.

Then the inevitable happened. Noses began to twitch and snuffling sounds could be heard. A loud indignant voice boomed, "It's pee! He peed on us!" Looks of disgust and horror were quickly replaced by anger and belligerence.

The next morning a huge van showed up at the University Veterinary School where I was in residence. Inside was the accused elephant, Bubbles. After hearing of Bubbles' transgression, we thought it possible that he might have cystitis—a bladder infection. That would explain why every time he sat for his act, pressure on his inflamed bladder sphincter resulted in the audience getting sprayed with urine—not exactly conducive to repeat business.

It was my job to get a urine sample to confirm the diagnosis. Can you imagine the process of getting a urine sample from an elephant? You have to have a *big* imagination. Well, getting the sample is a whole other story, but suffice it to say, I got one. Bubbles did have cystitis, and I told the trainer we'd have to treat him for at least three weeks.

The trainer decided to have Bubbles castrated while he was at the hospital. He thought Bubbles was becoming increasingly unpredictable with maturity, and castration might decrease his aggressiveness. Guess whose job it was to castrate him?

Now, until then I'd never given much thought to what castrating an elephant would be like. But, suddenly I realized that you never see anything hanging down between an elephant's legs. That's because, in God's wisdom, everything is internal—to prevent injury (or maybe jealousy).

Bubbles had to be anesthetized, of course, and something the size of a stove pipe was put down his trachea to deliver the gases. While sedated, he had to be turned from side to side every ten minutes, or the weight of his body would collapse his lungs.

To perform the surgery, you make an incision and insert your whole arm until you feel the rope-like throbbing vessels, which have to be tied off—blindly. You can't see what you're doing—everything has to be done by feel. Just think how difficult it would be to tie two square knots (by feel alone) in a tiny space. And then visualize how difficult it would be to cut between the two knots—again, blindly—realizing that if you didn't tie the knots tight enough, this expensive and majestic animal could easily bleed to death. And then, remember, this has to be done twice, further pushing the safety envelope.

As I worked, it seemed like the whole staff was watching. When I made the first cut between the tied-off vessels, we collectively held our breath. No one stirred or took their eyes off the incision site—would there be a gush of blood, spelling disaster? The moment could rival any critical moment in an action scene of a movie—like when they cut the bomb wires, which might not have been correctly disarmed. As moments passed and no blood was seen, people started breathing and speaking again—until the next side. Then utter stillness. I swear, hearts stopped beating—at least mine did. But, Bubbles did just fine, on both counts.

෨ ෨෨ ෨෨ ෨෨

Cystitis, infection or inflammation of the bladder, is very common in cats. We used to have the erroneous idea that ash in their food was responsible—cat guardians would go to great lengths to buy the food with the lowest ash content. This was a problem, because "ash" is another name for minerals that are, of course, necessary, and decreasing the minerals didn't stop the cystitis. We now know that urine that is too alkaline causes cystitis, and most commercial foods have started to add products to make the urine more acidic. One of the things you can do at home is not to leave food out all day for your cat; feed him only twice a day, morning and evening. Frequent feeding further alkalizes the urine, possibly leading to the formation of calculi and urinary blockages and inflammations. Cats, as carnivores, are meant to eat infrequently and have fasts in between.

⊚◟◟⊚◟◟⊚◟◟

In my practice, whenever the subject of cats urinating is introduced, questions about litter boxes come up. Here are a few helpful hints:

It is said that the factors most important for real estate, where a murderer should dispose of a body, and where a person should place a litter box are location, location, and location. In a multilevel home, you should have boxes on every floor of the house. Litter boxes should be away from the cat's food and water—cats don't like to excrete in their eating areas. Some cats like to urinate in one box and defecate in another, so be sure you have adequate numbers of boxes.

The construction of the litter box is important. Many cats won't use covered boxes; it makes them feel vulnerable, as if they couldn't flee if they chose to. If older cats are having accidents, construct a ramp to the box so they can get in and out more easily.

Which litter material does your cat prefer? It's usually not the perfumed material that their human guardians prefer (some cats are even allergic to the products). Paulette Cooper and Paul Noble, in *277 Secrets*

*Your Cat Wants You to Know,* report that we can tell how much a cat likes a particular litter by how much he digs in it. The happier the cat is with litter, the more he will dig. If your cat is digging outside the litter box, chances are he doesn't like the litter material inside the box. They suggest you put two litter boxes side by side with different litter and see which one your cats uses the most.

Cooper and Noble also have some suggestions for cats with bad aim —when feces or urine ends outside of the box. You can try a bigger box or one with higher sides. You can put the litter box inside a larger cardboard box or place the box on Astroturf or newspaper. They also have a great idea on how to stop cats from urinating in the bathtub: Leave an inch of water in there so that the next time he jumps in, he'll have an unpleasant surprise.

Some tips for cleaning up accidents: Scope mouthwash is good at getting urine smells out of the carpet, while Sink the Stink, available in dive/scuba shops, is remarkably effective.

෩෨෧෨෧෨

Let's not leave dogs out of the discussion of urinating. Do you know why male dogs cock or lift their legs while urinating?

As puppies, both males and females squat to urinate, but at puberty, around the age of eight or nine months, male dogs begin to lift one back leg when squirting their jet of urine. The raised leg is stretched out stiffly, with the body of the dog angled so that the stream of liquid is aimed sideways, instead of downward into the ground below.

This procedure doesn't seem to be driven by male hormones. Male dogs that have been neutered before reaching puberty will start to cock their legs at the same age as those that are fully sexually active. The urine will leave messages about the sexual condition of the dogs, because sex hormones are excreted in the urine. Also present are special, personal secretions from the male's accessory glands, giving each scent deposit the quality of an identity label.

One of the reasons that dogs mark vertical surfaces rather than the ground is to keep the scent signals as fresh as possible. Urine on the ground makes it more vulnerable to disturbance. Also, marking on a vertical surface brings the urine scents up to the nose level of other dogs, making the scents more conspicuous.

Marking with urine is a type of "time-sharing" of territory. It allows all of the canine population to know who passes through and when. Studies of free-roaming village dogs reveal that they spend as much as two to three hours every day checking all the scent marks in their territory. Although this means the expenditure of a great deal of time and effort, it nevertheless gives every dog in a particular village a complete dog map of the area, with information about local canine population size, movements, sexual condition, and identity. What can the dog do who can't find a fire hydrant or tree? Get a lawn, little doggie.

About a quarter of all female dogs raise one back leg when urinating, but the way it is done differs from the male's action. In the female leg-raising, one of the back legs is lifted up underneath her body, rather than stretched out to one side. The result is that her urine still falls on the ground rather than on a vertical surface.

❧ ❧ ❧ ❧ ❧

In regards to feces, cats don't bury their feces because they are fastidious, but as a way of decreasing their odor display. Feces-burying is the act of a subordinate cat, fearful of its social standing. Proof of this was found when feral cats were studied. It was discovered that dominant tomcats actually placed their feces on little "advertising" mounds or any other raised points in the environment where the odor could be wafted abroad to maximum effect. Only the weaker, more subdued cats hid their feces.

Our companion cats always bury their feces because they consider us the dominant cat. We are physically stronger than they are and control their food source. Burying the feces does not, of course, completely switch off the odor signal, but it does reduce it drastically. In this way the cat can continue to announce its presence through its scents, but not to the extent that it transmits a serious threat. So, what does it tell you if *your* cat doesn't bury its feces? You're right—he thinks he's the "cat's meow" and you, well, you're just another thing to toy with. ☀

## Make Sure the Snake
## in the House is Not a
## "Beau" Constrictor

As a veterinarian, I take care of injured and orphaned wildlife. I often keep the animals at home to prevent them from transmitting diseases to my patients at the hospital, plus wild animals seem happier with less noise and fewer people about. Over the years, I have found the spare bathroom to be a convenient place to keep them. This led to an incident involving Gordon, who was then my boyfriend.

I was in the main bathroom "freshening up." I had warned Gordon that if he had to use the other bathroom, he should remember that I had wildlife in there. I told him there were two flying squirrels that were out of their cages so they could get practice jumping around prior to being released, so he should be sure not to leave the toilet seat up or they could drown.

He entered the bathroom and was startled to see—and smell—so many creatures, large and small. He saw newspapers on the floor with a fawn curled up in the corner. Two flying squirrels were climbing about on a big branch lying diagonally across the room. There was a box full of baby birds, a jack rabbit in the shower, an empty cage (probably from the squirrels), and an empty aquarium (from some past visitor, no doubt).

Since he had time to burn, he decided to sit upon the throne, as is a man's right, to do his business in a leisurely fashion and read a magazine.

The fawn came over and started suckling in earnest on his knee. He gently pushed him away, but the noise awakened the birds; they started cheeping loudly and persistently, demanding to be fed. This startled the jack rabbit, causing him to start jumping and banging into the glass shower doors. As Gordon tried to reassure the rabbit that he wasn't a fox, one of the squirrels jumped onto his head. Not to be outdone, the other one jumped on his lap. They proceeded to chase each other using his naked legs as tree trunks. I'm sure you realize that they can scramble up and down trees because they have hook-like claws. A phenomenon not so much interesting as intensely painful, from Gordon's perspective.

So amid his shrieks of pain, he attempted to catch the squirrels and relocate them. The fawn began suckling his knee again—absolutely certain there was a nipple somewhere. The rabbit renewed its kamikaze attempts to crash through the glass shower door, and the baby birds were screeching like fishwives to get his attention. He prepared to abdicate his throne, when he felt a bumping on his derriere. He peered between his legs and found himself jumping even higher than the rabbit, heard himself screaming, and felt his heart pounding a heretofore never-experienced rhythm. There was a snake rearing up out of the toilet bowl!

I dashed through the door, obviously relieved when I saw that all the animals were okay. I told him that it was just a harmless corn snake, but

**177**

he yelled, "There is no such thing as a harmless snake in the toilet bowl!"

One of the attributes of corn snakes is their ability to rise up into the air like cobras (it fooled Gordon!). The missing resident of the aquarium had managed to raise up and push the lid off. Seeing the dark hole between the toilet bowl and the seat, it must have slithered in—and probably was none too pleased with Gordon's fouling up its new den.

Well, to tell you the rest of the story—Gordon *did* continue to date this crazy vet girlfriend—even married me, in fact. But you can bet he insisted on one thing—we will always have separate bathrooms!

ᕲᕲᕲᕲᕲ

Snakes and other reptiles need to hire a public relations firm—they have a bad image in our society and get blamed for many things that aren't their fault. One such "bad thing" is salmonellosis.

Have you ever gone out to eat and several hours later became very ill—fever, diarrhea, vomiting, and stomach pain? Sound like food poisoning? Did you know that most food poisoning is salmonellosis, caused by the ingestion of food contaminated with salmonella bacteria, an organism found in many creatures, especially chickens, reptiles, and insects?

Salmonella contamination has become a huge problem in our society, especially from poultry and eggs. We all know that poultry and eggs have to be cooked to kill this bacteria. (Alas, what is to happen to the Caesar salad that is traditionally made with a raw egg?) The mistake most people make is cutting up chicken in the kitchen, then reusing the knife and cutting board for other things, contaminating them.

When people with reptiles for companion animals come down with salmonellosis, the poor animals are always blamed, even though the humans probably contracted the bacteria from poorly cooked poultry or eggs, not from handling their reptiles. Do you remember the little red-eared turtles that used to be so popular as pets? The Food and Drug Administration banned the sale of them in the United States in 1975. They said they harbored salmonella, and children were getting infected by putting the turtles in their mouths (yuk!), so they banned the sale of any red-eared turtles smaller than four inches (small enough to be put into the mouth). The FDA elected not to require testing and treating of the positive turtles (which makes more sense to me), but to ban them entirely. It is interesting to note that the turtle industry, primarily based in Louisiana, ships over 6 million turtles yearly to Europe. Have you seen any headlines about all the European kids coming down with salmonella from putting turtles in their mouths? Neither have I, so it's obvious that the turtles weren't causing the salmonellosis in children. Is there anyone from the FDA reading this?

Ron Siebeling, Ph.D., developed a procedure ten years ago for decontaminating turtle eggs of salmonella. The procedure involves removing turtle eggs from the soil where they are laid and placing them in a clean, laboratory-like environment. The shells are sterilized and treated with gentamicin, an antibiotic known for its ability to kill salmonella bacteria (this would also work for iguanas and other egg-laying reptiles). But the FDA is worried about the development of a gentamicin-resistant strain of salmonella, so no lifting of the turtle ban is in sight.

Good hygiene is important if you own a reptile (or any animal, for that matter). Salmonella is spread to people usually through fecal-oral contact, so it's vital that you wash your hands after handling your reptile. It's also not a good idea to let the reptile walk across countertops or be in other areas where it may have close contact with people. And their dirty water shouldn't be dumped into the same sink where the dishes are washed, since this could contaminate the dishware.

๑ ๑๑ ๑๑ ๑๑

There is one more thing doctors advise reptile guardians: No kissing! Normally a couple of Xs represents a couple of kisses—but in the case of reptiles, it means "double-crossed" again. ✳

# They Said *What?*

Some last thoughts about talking to animals. Just as in communication between people, when you're "listening" to your companion animal, don't be impatient—listen to everything he has to say. An incident that demonstrates this point occurred a couple of years ago. We'd had two emergencies on top of an already full schedule. My receptionist was helping a technician take an X ray, so I answered the phone. "Dr. Pasten," I said. "How can I help you?"

"Oh, Dr. Laura, I'm so glad you answered. My husband is away, and I'm breeding my mare for the first time. How long do I leave the stallion in with her?"

Two other phone lines were ringing, and I knew the answer would take some time. "Just a minute," I said, expecting to put her on hold.

"Thank you," she said and hung up.

As you can see, being impatient can cause a great deal of miscommunication. Especially when talking to animals, we need to keep our minds clear for a couple of minutes after each image they send to us, to be sure more aren't coming. It's not like verbal communication, where as soon as one person stops talking, the other one can talk or leave.

As a Whisperer, you can either be your animal's healer or her cause of sickness. How is that possible? Albert Schweitzer, the great humanitarian and healer, said that the good doctor simply awakens the physician within the patient. A healer, by influencing the mind of the patient (together with veterinary medicine or surgery to directly affect the body), activates the "physician within." Therefore, if an animal is emotionally attached to her healer, she is more likely to benefit than if she were not attached or were being treated by a stranger. That's right—you, the guardian, can be the best healer (with the aid of your veterinarian) for your companion animal.

But it can work the other way, too, for companion animals and their guardians develop a psychic or telepathic sensitivity to each other. The sensitivity encompasses not only a responsiveness to cues that can be picked up by the five senses, but also to those that are intangible. People's thoughts, emotions, and behavior can make their animals sick as well as heal them.

That's why companion animals often have the same health problems as their guardians—itchy dogs often have itchy guardians, and overweight cats often have overweight humans. Animals often contract the very disease the guardians feared they'd themselves get. Animals mirror the guardian's own pattern of expectation. Why this happens is not so clear, unless you realize that animals probably do not readily distinguish where thoughts originate. Rather, they may just soak up whatever is sent their way, including the mental pictures transmitted by the guardian as he thinks, "I'm tired," or "I'm afraid I have cancer." Your companion animal absorbs all of these images of sickness, and often will exhibit the symptoms you were thinking about.

I have seen many animals become ill because of problems in the household, or because for one reason or another they lose a former privilege (such as being allowed on the furniture or getting special treats). Animals can get very upset by household conflicts that do not involve them, because they pick up the emotional energy created by the tensions without understanding that they are not to blame. Psychologists attribute similar processes to young children, who often blame themselves for their parents' arguments.

If your companion animal becomes ill after a lifestyle change (including your going on vacation, getting married, or the animal's loss of a playmate), ask yourself whether she is reacting to a loss of attention. If an animal suddenly receives less attention, she may not understand the reason. Instead, she may feel threatened, even fearing that her very survival is endangered. The animal may feel that she doesn't count anymore, that she has incurred disfavor. So what can happen? Due to the combination of stress and insecurity, your companion may develop a minor symptom like excessive licking or scratching (which could remind her of the security of her mother's licking when she was a baby). You, the guardian, immediately get upset. You run over, pet her, and, in an anxious voice, lavish her with concern and attention. This response cannot only transmit the image of sickness to the animal (thereby perpetuating the symptoms), but also gives your attention-starved companion a definite "stroke" for acting sick.

So be sure to try to control your communications, both verbal and nonverbal, and the thought processes and images you share with your companion animal. As mentioned throughout this book, use your common sense, and try to understand things from the animal's point of view.

The key word to keep in mind for all these techniques for "talking with the animals" is *open-mindedness*. It is very important to clear your mind of any preconceived ideas, because they can be self-limiting. The best way to approach new ideas such as these is to have an attitude that Tellington-Jones describes as the "gourd head" state. The concept comes from a novel she once read about an amazing samurai in fourteenth-century Japan, a kind of knight-protector of the realm, who won all of his battles in spite of the fact that he was blind. His secret, when challenged, was to visualize his head as a hollow gourd empty of all thoughts and images. Because nothing in his mind colored or blocked his incoming perceptions, all of his senses became super-sensitive to the slightest nuance of what was happening around him—a kind of second sight. Keeping a "gourd head," experiment with some of the communication techniques such as T-touch and creating images to send to your animals, and you too can develop a kind of second sight.

Well, Whisperer wannabees, let's review. To be a Whisperer, we must have a knowledge of animals, how they evolved, and why they do what they do. We need to be able to create and send visual images in our minds in order to communicate with animals. We must become familiar with holistic medicine and techniques like T-touch. We need to use common sense as well as scramble our senses: listen with our fingers; see with our gut; and think with our heart. Are you ready? You have to start sometime. Like Will Rogers said, "Even if you're on the right track, you'll get run over if you just sit there!" Let's listen in right now.

⊘◎ ◎⊘ ◎⊘

I see two cats over there. Let's try to listen to their conversation. Cat 1: "That's not a canary, it's green." Cat 2: "You never know; it might not be ripe yet!" Cat 1: "Let's get out of here; let's go to Cat's Fifth Avenue and check out the computers." Cat 2: "Good idea; there's often a mouse nearby." Cat 1: "I heard there was an ad in the newspaper for that Persian cat's kittens." Cat 2: "Oh, yeah? What did it say?" Cat 1: "It said, 'Free kittens. Mother—snowy Persian; father—from a nice neighborhood!'"

⊘◎ ◎⊘ ◎⊘

And over there are two skunks talking on a smellular phone. Let's listen in. Skunk 1: "What happened when your sister mated with that boomerang?" Skunk 2: "She got a nasty smell she couldn't get rid of, but I heard she got a Pewlitzer prize." Skunk 1: "Do you know what the difference is between a person with ESP and a skunk?" Skunk 2: "Yeah, one's got a sixth sense; the other a sick scent."

❧ ❧ ❧ ❧ ❧

Down the road are two horses interacting. Horse 1: "Remember me?" Horse 2: "I don't remember your face, but your mane is familiar."

❧ ❧ ❧ ❧ ❧

And what is that little, pretty flying thing over there. It's saying, "Hmmmmmmmmmm—choo. Hmmmmmmmmm—choo." Oh, I see, it's a hummingbird with a cold.

❧ ❧ ❧ ❧ ❧

What are those two bulls saying? Bull 1: "When I fall in love it will be for heifer." Bull 2: "How about that heifer over yonder?" Bull 1: "Her? She's so fat, she has her own zip code!"

❧ ❧ ❧ ❧ ❧

We can even understand those two snakes now. Snake 1: "Are we supposed to be poisonous?" Snake 2: "Why do you ask, my slithery friend?" Snake 1: "Because I've just bitten my lip." Snake 1: "Do you know why that tortoise crossed the road?" Snake 2: "Yes, to get to the Shell station."

◈◈◈◈◈

Two dogs are talking. Dog 1: "Did you know that Poncho has two penises?" Dog 2: "Yes, I heard he calls one Jose and the other Hose-B." Dog 1: "Do you know what the male dog said to a spayed female? Thanks for nothin'."

◈◈◈◈◈

And what do you get if you cross a germ with a comedian? That's right. . . . sick jokes! I realize *these* are sick jokes, but they are intended to put a smile on your face (or a groan on your lips) as you prepare to try your skills at communicating with animals. Listen with all your senses, including your common sense, the existing knowledge of your body, and the wisdom of your soul. Have fun with it! And drop me a line, telling me what new insights and experiences you've had since you too became a Whisperer. ☀

# Acknowledgments

Gordon Hellwig, Jr., my husband, for his love and support (both emotionally and financially) and for providing me with such fascinating experiences to write about.

My parents, Rex and Jean Jeppsen, and my brother, Larry Brakovich, for their encouragement and belief in me and for not leaving me in a snowbank to die after discovering I was a weird kid who had to surround herself with every creature imaginable.

My aunt, Betty Lawson, for her quirky sense of humor, which rubbed off on me.

Don Low, for his Schnauzer story (now you know who's to blame!).

Mary Jane Ryan, my editor, for taking the time to speak at the Asilomar Writing Conference, then daring to give a contract to this first-time author.

Maxine Shore, editor and professor, for her help and advice. And since she's now *up there* with Tybo, maybe she can read this book to him before she begins her angelic writing class.

Margaret White, both a Whisperer and a Healer of all creatures great and small, with and without tails.

Carmel Writers' Group: Joan and Don Miller, McKenzie Moss, Lisa Watson, Gretta Kopp, Melodie Bahou, Nancy Gardner, Mary Clarkson, Maggie Hardy, Mary Barker. (McKenzie, you'll notice there are *no* adverbs on this page, and Joan, I think you should do the audio to this book.)

Beth and Walt Weissman for their advice—and for introducing me as an author before I really was . . . an author, that is.

Rachel De Velder and Jo Smiley, for their many skills and abilities in keeping my office from being classified as a Disaster Area.

# Bibliography

The author wishes to gratefully acknowledge the books cited here. They were very helpful to me, and I think they would be useful sources for those of you who are aspiring Whisperers. Items marked with an asterisk (*) were of particular value in writing this book.

Anderson, Niki. *What My Cat Has Taught Me about Life*. Tulsa OK: Honor Books, Inc., 1997.

Barry, Dave. *Dave Barry's Bad Habits*. New York: Henry Holt and Company, Inc., 1985.

*Boone, J. Allen *Kinship with All Life*. New York: HarperSanFrancisco, 1976.

Coren, Stanley. *The Intelligence of Dogs: Canine Consciousness and Capabilities*. New York: The Free Press, 1994.

Cooper, Paulette, and Paul Noble. *277 Secrets Your Cat Wants You to Know*. Berkeley CA: Ten Speed Press, 1997.

*Cooper, Paulette, and Paul Noble *277 Secrets Your Dog Wants You to Know*. Berkeley CA: Ten Speed Press, 1995.

Evans, Nicholas. *The Horse Whisperer.* New York: Dell Publishing, 1995.

Greene, David. *Your Incredible Cat.* New York: Galahad Books, 1984.

Kilcommons, Brian, and Sarah Wilson. *Good Owners, Great Dogs.* New York: Warner Books, 1992.

*Masson, Jeffrey Moussaieff. *Dogs Never Lie About Love.* New York: Crown Publishers, Inc., 1997.

The Monks of New Skete. *How to Be Your Dog's Best Friend: A Training Manual for Dog Owners.* Boston: Little, Brown and Company, 1978.

*Morris, Desmond. *Catlore.* New York: Crown Publishers, Inc., 1987.

*Morris, Desmond. *Illustrated Catwatching.* New York: Crescent Books, 1994.

*Morris, Desmond. *Illustrated Dogwatching.* New York: Crescent Books, 1996.

*Pitcairn, Richard, D.V.M., and Susan Hubble, M.S. *Dr. Pitcairn's Complete Guide to Natural Health for Dogs and Cats.* Emmaus, PA: Rodale Press, Inc., 1995.

*Stein, Diane. *Natural Healing for Dogs and Cats.* Freedom, CA: The Crossing Press, 1993.

## Bibliography

*Tellington-Jones, Linda, with Sybil Taylor. *The Tellington T-Touch.* New York: Penguin Books USA, Inc., 1992.

Wright, Michael, and Sally Walters. *The Book of the Cat.* New York: Summit Books, 1980.

# About the Author

Dr. Laura Pasten is a world-renowned multimedia veterinarian. She has traveled extensively with her most famous patient, Morris the 9-Lives Cat as a spokesperson for the American Veterinary Medical Association. Her AAHA-certified veterinary hospital has earned her national recognition and has received many awards. She was named Most Admired Woman of the Decade in 1994 by the American Biographical Institute, International Woman of the Year in 1995 and 1997, and received the Lifetime Achievement award for her contributions to the field of veterinary medicine. Her video, *How Smart Is Your Puppy?*, is available through Direct Books Service, 1-800-776-2665.

Dr. Pasten, her husband, and her menagerie of furry family members reside in Carmel, California. Contact her via Conari Press, 2550 Ninth Street, Suite 101, Berkeley, California 94710.

Conari Press, established in 1987, publishes books on topics
ranging from psychology, spirituality, and women's history to sexuality,
parenting, and personal growth. Our main goal is to publish quality
books that will make a difference in people's lives—both how
we feel about ourselves and how we relate to one another.

Our readers are our most important resource, and we value your
input, suggestions, and ideas. We'd love to hear from you—
after all, we are publishing books for you!

To request our latest book catalog, or to be added to
our mailing list, please contact:

CONARI PRESS
2550 Ninth Street, Suite 101
Berkeley, California
94710-2551

800-685-9595      510-649-7175
fax: 510-649-7190
e-mail: Conari@conari.com
www.conari.com